Percy H. Fitzgerald

The Life of Mrs. Catherine Clive

With an Account of her Adventures on and off the Stage

Percy H. Fitzgerald

The Life of Mrs. Catherine Clive
With an Account of her Adventures on and off the Stage

ISBN/EAN: 9783337177713

Printed in Europe, USA, Canada, Australia, Japan

Cover: Foto ©Raphael Reischuk / pixelio.de

More available books at **www.hansebooks.com**

THE LIFE OF

MRS.

CATHERINE CLIVE

WITH AN ACCOUNT OF HER

Adventures on and off the Stage

A ROUND OF HER CHARACTERS

TOGETHER WITH HER CORRESPONDENCE

BY

PERCY FITZGERALD,

M.A., F.S.A.

LONDON:

A. READER, ORANGE STREET, HOLBORN.

1888.

Inscribed to

Joseph Knight.

PREFACE.

THE task of calling up the images of departed actors who have passed beyond the recollection of even the oldest playgoers, seems all but hopeless. With the most diligent examination of contemporary impressions the result is barren enough; for too often the reporter, supposing he have felt the inspiration, lacks the power to reproduce his impressions. It indeed needs ability of the highest order to touch this instrument; and it may be said that we have but two critics who have left breathing portraits of the actors of their time, namely, Colley Cibber and Charles Lamb. Language fails, save in the case of such masters, to give an idea of the style, the sympathetic graces, and the indefinable charm which render an actor popular, and secure him his hold over an audience; and this, though not exactly described, is shadowed forth in the magical lines of Shakespere—

> "As when the well graced actor leaves the scene,
> The eye is often idly bent on him that enters next."

B

Here we recognise this mysterious awe left on our minds
by the true player—the strange undefined mystery, with the
sense of a revelation beyond the hackneyed round of daily
life. We must therefore resign ourselves in the case of
departed performers to such accurate registers of their
manner and methods, or what is vulgarly called "business,"
as diligent observers have collated. Of such records there
is an abundance. It is not unnatural that the public,
thus driven to content itself with this superficial and
imperfect ideal, should have formed some hasty and
erroneous conception of the old favourites. It reads as
it runs—it has not time, nor is it able to make nice
discrimination of character—all must be black or white.
It has thus settled for itself that "Davy" Garrick was a
close, clever, and knowing fellow; that "Peg" Woffington
was a tender-hearted, rollicking Irish girl—one of a class
"who is no one's enemy but their own;" that Kemble was
a solemn prig, always uttering stately periods; that the
person with whom we are directly concerned—Mrs. Clive—
was a pert being, of an impudent chamber-maid cast. These
popular judgments are more or less erroneous, for the
three persons in question were almost the reverse of what
they were supposed to have been. Woffington had nothing
frivolous in her nature, but was saving, thoughtful, and
conscientious in her profession, which she never neglected.

Garrick was liberal to a degree; Kemble often sat up, whole nights over the bottle, and was excellent company. In the case of Mrs. Clive, it has been settled according to the conventional view,—that she was pert, impudent and petulant. Dr. Doran is accountable for this use of misleading epithets, speaking with affectionate sympathy of imaginary "Pegs" and "Kittys" as though he had sat with them. We are introduced to Kitty Clive, and see her squaring her elbows and wrangling with Davy. Mrs. Clive was a rather prosaic person, one of those who make their profession and its earnings the first object of their life; she was plain, and had few adventures in her life; she had a warm temper, she knew her value to the theatre in vivacious, "bustling" characters, and resented any interference with her duties. From her writing she appears to have been ill educated, but she had what Dr. Johnson would have called a "strong bottom of sense." It has become a common-place to speak of her bad spelling, but this defect mended with years. She will be found to be a genuine woman, sincere, firm, and fast in her friendships; while her downright character was exhibited in many episodes scarcely known, and which will be found interesting.

In the following pages will be found the first full and formal account of the life and adventures of this accom-

plished actress.   Many new incidents have been discovered,
while various curious little episodes illustrating the independence or forwardness of our actress, are here, for the
first time, recounted.   Some new letters are now given,
together with much that illustrates her style of performance
in various characters.

The Life of Mrs. Catherine Clive.

CHAPTER I.

The Raftor Family. — Kitty Introduced to the Stage. — Engaged by Cibber.—Her Success in "Love in a Riddle."—Her Ballad Singing.—Great Fiasco of the Piece.—Her Marriage to Mr. Clive.

MRS. CATHERINE CLIVE—or "Kitty Clive" as she was familiarly known to her associates—one of the brightest and most spirited of actresses—came of an Irish family, named Raftor, settled at Kilkenny. The obligations of the English Stage to that country are extraordinary. The names of Delane, Quin, Barry, Mossop, Sheridan, Macklin, the infant Roscius, Betty, Cooke, Macready, Barry Sullivan; with Woffington, Clive, Bellamy, Catley, Miss Farren, Miss O'Neil, and Mrs. Nesbitt, make up quite a galaxy of talent, and indeed leave little more to the other countries than the great leaders, Kembles, Siddons, and Kean, with our own living tragedian Irving. Not less remarkable are the dramatic writers who could equip such a company with plays worthy of their talents:— Steele, Farquhar, Goldsmith, Sheridan, O'Keefe, Sheridan Knowles, and many more. Scotland so gifted in writers of song and fiction is strangely deficient in this line.

Anything that we know of the Raftor family, and of the early life of its gifted daughter we owe altogether to the worthy Chetwood, who was long connected with the Dublin Theatre, having written a little collection of sketches of the performers he knew. He possessed a quaint, simple style, as will be evident from his account of our heroine :

"This celebrated natural actress was the daughter of Mr. William Raftor, a gentleman born in the City of Kilkenny, Ireland. The father of her father was possessed of a considerable paternal estate in the county where he was born ; but the parents of our actress being unhappily attached to the unfortunate King James the Second, the late Revolution gave it, among many others to the Crown. Mr. James Raftor, her brother, went over to Ireland some years ago, in order to solicit for his grandfather's fortune, but did not meet with success. Mr. William Raftor the father was tied to the law ; however when King James was in Ireland, he entered into his service, and after the decisive Battle of the Boyne in the year 1690, he followed his master's fortune, and by his merit obtained a captain's commission in the service of Louis the Fourteenth ; but gaining a pardon, with many other gentlemen in his condition, he came to England where he married Miss Daniel, daughter of an eminent citizen on Fish Street Hill, with whom he had a handsome fortune. By her he had a numerous issue. Miss Catherine was born in 1711. She had an early genius for the stage, for she told me when she was about twelve years old, Miss Johnston (afterwards Mrs. Theo. Cibber, another rising genius, if death had not overtaken her in the prime of youth), and she used to tag after the celebrated Mr. Wilks (her own words) wherever they saw him in the streets, and gape at him as a wonder.

Miss Raftor had a facetious turn of humour and infinite spirit, with a voice and manner in singing songs of pleasantry peculiar to herself."

These touches bring the young girl vividly before us. The handsome fortune of Miss Daniel must have been speedily dissipated by Captain Raftor, for we shall find the whole burden of supporting him and his family cast upon the young actress, who was all through life remarkable for her family affection.

Through Miss Johnston, in whose company she used to " tag after " Mr. Wilks—a pleasantly expressive phrase— she became acquainted with Theo. Cibber — that extraordinary and impish member of the profession. Miss Johnston was Theo.'s first wife, and whose loss he bewailed. "Should men say, for instance, I used my first dear and well-beloved wife, of ever blessed memory, J—n—y C——, with ill usage; should they affirm, that when her all pale and breathless corpse was laid in the coffin, and I, with sobs and tears and interjected sighs, had moaned to many a witness, my too unhappy fate, yet that same night had a brace of Drurian doxies vile in the same house?"

There is an account given by Lee Lewes of "Kitty's" original connection with the stage—which has a curious probability—but which does not fit with the received accounts.

" She was originally," he says, " servant to Miss Eleanor Knowles, afterwards Mrs. Young, mother to the present Sir George Young and Mr. Thomas Young, who in 1774 came out at Covent Garden Theatre in *Macheath*, which he performed some nights with much celebrity. When Mrs. Clive lived with Mrs. Knowles, who then lodged at Mrs. Snell's, a fan painter in Church Row, Houndsditch, Mr.

Watson, many years boxkeeper at Drury Lane and Rich-
mond, kept the Bell Tavern, directly opposite to Mrs.
Snell's. At this house was held the Beefsteak Club, insti-
tuted by Mr. Beard, Mr. Dunstall, Mr. Woodward, &c.
Kitty Raftor, being one day *washing the steps of the house*,
and singing, the windows of the club room being open,
they were instantly crowded by the company, who were all
enchanted with her natural grace and simplicity. This
circumstance alone led her to the stage, under the auspices
of Mr. Beard and Mr. Dunstall." . . I have given the
above anecdote as I received it from Mr. Thomas Young.

There is in this, an air of possibility; but, it will be
seen that there are improbabilities. It is unlikely that the
daughter of a gentleman and an officer, would go out as a
servant or wash steps. Nor was the club in question likely
to have its meetings so far east as Houndsditch. It may
be, however, that there is a foundation for the story,
and that the girl was in place of service, as companion
perhaps, and was overheard singing by the actors in question. Such legends are often questioned, but there is
generally some basis of truth in them.

Scarcely desirable, as an acquaintance for a young girl,
was Theo. Cibber's sister Charlotte, afterwards Mrs. Clarke
—a strange, wild, half-mad creature—who had a disastrous
fate, which she herself has recounted.

"These talents," adds Chetwood, "Mrs. Theo. Cibber
and I (we were all at that time living together in one
house) thought a sufficient passport to the theatre—we
recommended her to the Laureate. Her teacher in music
was the luckless Henry Carey, who is claimed by his friends
to have been the author of "God save the King"—or Queen
—as it may be. He is better known however as the author

of the ever popular "Sally in our Alley"—which pleased even the correct taste of Mr. Addison, and which " Kitty " must have often warbled under his direction.   We find her furnishing her talent to entertainments given for his benefit on several occasions.

Dr. Burney says she was a favourite with Handel, and was employed by him in his oratorios—singing in " Deborah." He however adds, that she was quite unsuited to serious or sacred music—which was indeed to be expected from a comic singer.   In the Garrick Club there is an important portrait of her which represents her with a rather plain but good-humoured face, buxom in figure—with a low dress, and which is characteristic of her taste, a scroll of music in her hand.   This piece displays some of Milton's lines set by Handel.

It was natural that in such companionship, she should soon have turned her eyes to the stage.   " We recommended her to the Laureate (Mr. Cibber) says Chetwood," whose infallible judgment soon found out her excellencies—and the moment he heard her sing, put her down in the list of performers at twenty shillings a week."   This modest salary is mentioned as something handsome for a beginner, but it was good considering the times.   Theatrical affairs at Drury Lane were not flourishing—and the prosperity which the three managers, Cibber, Wilks, and Doggitt had built up during many years, was showing signs of decay. Still it was an excellent school for her, as Wilks was there, whom, in her girlish days she had "tagged after," with Mills, Harper, Cibber himself—Mrs. Booth, Mrs. Oldfield, and Miss Porter, all sterling actors, and trained in the best traditions.   The progress of the young *debutante* was ratified.   "After this, like a bullet in the air, there was

c

no distinguishing the track till it came to its utmost execution "—the happy pointed phrase of the admiring Chetwood.

It has been stated that the first part allotted to the young postulant was that of the *Page* in "Mithridates, King of Pontus," a tragedy of the kind which Johnson happily styled the "Tig and Tiry" kind, from the usual Tigranes or Tiridates that figured in them. This part was specially garnished for her benefit, and we can suppose, set out in the bill—

> "Ismenes, page to Ziphanes *(with a song)* ...... MISS RAFTOR."

which she performed "in boy's clothes," says Chetwood, "with extraordinary applause." It is impossible, however, to discover the date of this successful *debut*. We are not even certain of the year, though the traditions which fixed it to 1728 may be accepted. Even the laborious Geneste, whom little escaped, could find no bill or newspaper to throw light on the matter. His earliest official record is a performance of "The Tempest," on January 2, 1729, in which she played *Dorinda*. By searching more carefully I have found some yet earlier performances. Thus, on October 12th, 1728, we have this programme :—

Not Acted this Season.
By His Majesty's Company of Comedians.
At the Theatre Royal in Drury Lane, To-morrow (being Satur-
day), the 12th day of October, will be presented a Tragedy
call'd
OTHELLO, MOOR OF VENICE.
The part of Othello to be performed by Mr. Elrington ; Iago by
Mr. Cibber; Cassio, Mr. Williams; Roderigo, Mr. Roberts;
Ludovico, Mr. Wm. Mills; Montano, Mr. Watson ; Desdemona,
Mrs. Thurmond ; Emilia, Mrs. Butler ; Bianca, Miss Raftor.

From this I fancy she must have appeared early in the
year. On the 22nd of the following month, Mr. Cibber
brought out the whole strength of his establishment in a
sort of Pantomime—competing with "Mr. Lunn," who was
exhibiting similar shows at the rival establishment.

N.B.—Not Acted these Two Years.

By His Majesty's Company of Comedians.

At the Theatre Royal in Drury Lane, this present Friday, being
the 22 day of November (1728), will be presented a Comedy,
call'd

ÆSOP:

The part of Æsop by Mr. Cibber.

To which will be added a New Dramatic Entertainment of
Dancing, in serious and grotesque characters, call'd

PERSEUS AND ANDROMEDA,
WITH THE
RAPE OF COLUMBINE; or, THE FLYING LOVERS:

In five different interludes, viz.: three serious and two comic;
the serious composed by Mons. Roger.

The part of Andromeda by Mrs. Booth; Perseus, Mr. Lally;
Mercury, Mr. Essex; Jupiter, Mr. Essex; Medusa, Mr. Thur-
mond; Two Gorgons, Mr. Houghton and Mr. Burney; Followers
of Perseus, Mr. Boval, Mr. Rainton, Mr. Houghton, Mr. Burney;
Attendants on Andromeda, Mrs. Houghton, Miss Walter, Miss
Lindar, Miss Robinson, sen.; The Houris of Sleep by Mrs.
Houghton, Miss Robinson, sen., Miss Walter, Miss Lindar;
Tritons, Mr. Thurmond, Mr. Essex, Mr. Houghton, Mr. Rainton;
Cephens, Mr. Fielding; Cassiopea, Mrs. Shireburn; Venus,
Miss Biddy; Minerva, Miss Raftor; Juno, Mrs. Shireburn;
Diana, Miss Smith; Sailors, Mr. Burney, Mr. Oates, Mr.
Wright, Mr. Welteribb, Mr. Burnet, and Mr. Grey; Cupid,
Miss Robinson, jun.; Doctor (Columbine's Father), Mr. Burney;
Pierrot (Doctor's Man), Mr. Roger; Mezetius (Columbine's
Lover), Mr. Ray; Harlequin (Mezetius' Man), Mr. Cibber, jun.;

Squire (designed for Columbine), Mr. R. Welterilf; Clown (Squire's Man), Mr. Weaver; Columbine (in love with Mezetius) Miss Robinson, sen.; Mopsophil (Columbine's Maid), Mrs. Walter.

The Scenery, Machines, Habits, entirely new.   All the Scenery painted by Mons. Devoto.*

Many of the performers, it will be seen, had to "double" and even "treble" the characters.   Minerva was not much of a part for Miss Raftor; but she was kept in company by so good a player as Mrs. Booth, who condescended to take part in this medley.

All readers know how potent was the effect of "His casual Sight of an old Play Bill" on Elia; and the faded characters of these frail records act like a spell, bringing us all into touch with the spirits of departed players.   Here is another connected with the opening of the young actress' career :—

ACTED BUT ONCE THESE TEN YEARS.
At the particular Desire of several Persons of Quality.
By His Majesty's Company of Comedians.

AT the Theatre Royal in Drury Lane, on Monday, the 29th day of July, will be reviv'd a Comedy, call'd

WHIG AND TORY: OR, THE DOUBLE DECEIT.
Revis'd by H. Aulius.

The Part of Sir John Indolent, by Mr. Griffin; Young Indolent, Mr. Cibber, jun.; Reyard, Mr. Watson; Sir Ronald Heartfree, Mr. Covey; Young Heartfree, Mr. Roberts; Philip, Mr. Berry; Cobblecase, Mr. Bridgwater; John, Mr. Fielding; Annita, Mrs. Butler; Charlotte, Mrs. Heron; Maria, Miss Raftor; Tamwoud, Mrs. Shirburn.

---

* During the elaborate preparations for this great show, young Leigh had his arm broke by the machinery being let down too rapidly at rehearsal.   It will be noted that Fielding's name appears in the cast.

With the original Prologue, to which, by desire, will be added the Opera call'd

PHŒBE; OR, THE BEGGAR'S WEDDING.

With Entertainment of Dancing. Between the Play and the Opera will be performed a piece of Music on the Violin by Mr. Clarke, accompanied by Mr. Magnes on the Harpsichord. Also a Voluntary by Mr. Magnes alone, being the first time of his performance in publick.

AT COMMON PRICES. To begin exactly at Seven o'clock.

N. B.—The House is extraordinarily cool. Plans to be had at Mr. Cook's, the Boxkeeper, in the Play House Passage. Printed Books of the Opera, as it is now performed, will be sold at the Theatre at 6d. each.—1729.

During this, her first season, we find her performing *Honoria* in "Love makes a Man," on January 26, 1729; *Valleria* in "The Rovers," on May 1; in "Wit without Money," on May 3, where she is set down as *Mrs.* Raftor; in "Duke and no Duke," on August 5; as *Arethusa* in "The Contrivances;" and as *Kitty* in "The Oxford Jilt," on January 9, 1730. On February 10, she appeared as *Rosella* in "The Constant Couple;" but it was not till August 6, 1731, that she made her first great hit as *Nell* in a version of "The Devil to Pay," altered and adapted by Coffey, where her boisterous vivacity made such an impression, not merely on the public, but on the management, that her salary was raised. In this part she became a prime favourite of the public. There were plenty of songs, and her rough, rattling, coarse humour in "The Cobbler's Wife" was much relished.

In a company which included such great performers, excellent lessons were to be learned. She there saw performed some of the most sterling pieces. She was given what seems to have been her first serious character, on

Jan. 2, 1729, when the "Tempest" was played, she taking the part of *Dorinda*, Mrs. Booth playing *Miranda*, to Wilks' *Ferdinand ;* but beyond this she seems to have played but seldom, though she must have appeared often.   For almost every night we find the advertisement: "with an entertainment of music and dancing."   Thus on October 30, 1729, "The Stratagem," that is "The Beaux Stratagem" was played, in which Oldfield and Porter had parts—and which was followed by "select pieces of music" between the acts."   Her characters during the rest of the season were *Honoria* in "Love Makes a Man ;" on January 26, *Valleria* in "The Rover," or "What d'ye call it; with a song by Miss Raftor."   On May 21, she also appeared in the version of "The Country Wife," and as *Arethusa* in a one-act farce, with several new songs.   On Jan. 9, 1730, she played the congenial part of *Kitty, the Oxford Jilt*, in the "Humours of Oxford."   In that month also, "The Tempest" was revived, on what was considered a scale of magnificence, "with scenes, machines, and other decorations suitable to the play"—and among these attractions so "suitable to the play," were the following :—"A Dance of the Four Winds, a Dance of Infernal Spirits, as performed before the Grand Signior, by the Eunuchs of the Seraglio, at the Bairiam Feast (!).   Also the song of 'Dear Pretty Youth,' as composed by the late Mr. Henry Purcell, to be sung in the character of *Dorinda* by Miss Raftor."   This wretched stuff shows to what the managers could condescend to draw an audience.   But on the production of a new piece by the manager, Colley Cibber, she was to have her first experience of the unruly manners of an audience.

Her bearing on this disastrous occasion was becoming her character and conscientious spirit.   "I remember," Chet-

wood tells us, " the first night of ' Love in a Riddle,' (which
was murdered the same year) which the hydra-headed mul-
titude resolved to worry without hearing, a custom with
authors of merit, when Miss Raftor came on in the part of
Phyllida ; the monstrous roar subsided, a person in the
stage-box next to my post, called out to his companion in
the following elegant style : ' *Zounds ! you take care, or
this charming little devil will save all !* ' "   This as we have
seen, she could not do.   The Prince of Wales was present on
the second night, but was no restraint on the turbulence of
the audience.   The piece, however, being cut down and
shortened, later became popular and was often acted.
There figured in it a "concealed courtier" played by Cibber
himself, with the inevitable *Damon* and *Corydon*.   In 1734
she was painted in the same character, by Van Bleeck, and a
large mezzotint was published from the picture, exhibiting a
graceful pastoral figure, with a face full of interest, if not
pretty.

A writer who knew her and whose recollections stretched
back a long way, describes her pastoral air exactly : " At
this period, the sprightliness and vivacity of her disposition,
and an appearance scarce more than infantine, pointed her
out as the proper representative of parts in which youth and
simplicity were to be personated."*   This air of infantine
innocence and simplicity is conveyed in the portrait.

DAMON AND PHYLLIDA.
CHARACTERS.

Arcus, a nobleman of great possessions in Arcadia...Mr. Winstone

Ægon (his friend)...Mr. Cole

Corydon, an old Shepherd ....Mr. Turbutt

---

* *European Magazine, 1784.*

Simon }	Simple brothers, in love with Phyllida {	... Mr. Miller
Mopsus }		... Mr. Oates
Damon, an inconstant.....................................Mr. Stoppelaer		
Phyllida, daughter to Corydon ....Mrs. Clive*		

The whole piece seems to have been written to bring out the young actress' powers. Most of the songs, which are set to old English tunes, are alloted to her, and seem to anticipate our music hall ditties. Thus :—

> What woman could do, I have tried, to be free,
>> Yet do all I can,
> I find I love him, and though he flies me,
>> Still—still he's the man.
> They tell me at once, he to twenty will swear :
> When vows are so sweet, who the falsehood can fear?
>> So when you've said all you can,
>> Still—still he's the man.

And again :—

> Give over your love, you great loobies,
>> I hate you both—you sir, and you too ;
> Did ever a brace of such boobies
>> The lass that detests them pursue ?
> Prepare then to hear my last sentence—
>> Before I'd wed either, much rather
> I'd stand on the stool of repentance,
>> And want for my bantling a father !

In later editions there is a pretty little etching by Van der Gucht, a well-known theatrical portrait painter, of Mrs. Clive in character, as a shepherdess, with crook, garlands, and a low dress.

Mr. Cibber thus relates the story of his *fiasco* :—

"After the vast success of that new species of dramatic poetry, 'The Beggar's Opera,' the year following, I was

* This is a later caste of characters, when the title of the piece had been altered.

so stupid, as to attempt something of the same kind upon quite a different foundation, that of recommending virtue and innocence, which I ignorantly thought might not have a less pretence to favour, than setting greatness and authority in a contemptible light. But behold how fondly I was mistaken! "Love in Riddle" (for so my new-fangled performance was called) was vilely damn'd and hooted at as so vain a presumption in the idle cause of virtue could deserve. Soon after this prohibition, my performance was to come upon the stage, at a time, when many people were out of humour at the late disappointment, and seemed willing to lay hold of any pretence of making a reprisal. Great umbrage was taken that I was permitted to have the whole town to myself, by this absolute forbiddance of what they had more mind to have been entertained with; and some few days before my bawble was acted, I was informed that a strong party would be made against it: this report I slighted, as not conceiving why it should be true, and when I was afterwards told what was the pretended provocation of this party, I slighted it. The report it seems that had run against me was this: That, to make way for the success of my own play, I had privately found means, or made interest, that the second part of 'The Beggar's Opera' might be suppressed. I had not considered, poor devil! that, from the security of a full pit, dunces might be critics, cowards valiant, and apprentices gentlemen! Whether any such were concerned in the murder of my play, I am not certain; for I never endeavoured to discover any one of its assassins; I cannot afford them a milder name, from their unmanly manner of destroying it. 'Tis true, it faintly held up its wounded head, a second day, and would have spoke for mercy, but

D

was not suffered. Not even the presence of a royal heir
apparent could protect it. But then I was reduced to be
serious with them; their clamour then became an insolence,
which I thought it my duty, by the sacrifice of any interest
of my own, to put an end to. I therefore quitted the
actor for the author, and stepping forward to the pit, told
them that since I found they were not inclined that this
play should go forward, I gave them my word, that after
this night, it should never be acted again : but that in the
mean time, I hoped they would consider in whose presence
they were, and for that reason at least, would suspend what
further marks of their displeasure they might imagine I
had deserved. At this there was a dead silence; and after
some little pause, a few civilized hands signified their
approbation. When the play went on, I observed about a
dozen persons of no extraordinary appearance sullenly
walked out of the pit; after which, every scene of it, while
uninterrupted, met with more applause than my best hopes
had expected. But it came too late : Peace to its manes !"

After this scene, there followed some monotonous years,
during which she was learning her profession, appearing
almost every night. Such diligence and industry soon
attracted attention. We find Aaron Hill, one of the
popular playwrights, the author or adaptor of ponderous
tragedies, in his "Zara," proposing to aid in bringing her
forward, classing her with Griffin and Harper. "I will be
sure," he wrote in January, 1733, "to write for you such
a farce as Mr. Booth described, and you shall have it in a
day or two. I had a thought that came in my head last
night, that will take into the compass of an act, the different
humour and strength of Harlequin, Mr. Stoppelaer, Miss
Raftor, Mr. Griffin, and Mr. Harper." He added, that one

great cause of want of success is that "things are not prepared on purpose to show the various talents in the company."

The attractive Miss Raftor, when she had been two or three years on the stage, was now to captivate a sober gentleman of good family, who married her. This was Mr. George Clive, a barrister without practice, brother to Sir Edward Clive, one of the Barons of the Exchequer, and nephew to another judge of the same family.   It was "a good match," the Clives being an old Hereford family; the famous Robert, Lord Clive, was second cousin to Mr. George Clive.   The marriage is said to have taken place in 1732, but the exact date is not known.   The bills however seem to furnish some evidence, for we find that on October 3rd, 1733, "Rule a Wife and have a Wife" was performed, in which "Miss Raftor" played; while on the 5th she appears of a sudden as "Mrs. Clive, formerly Miss Raftor."   We might fairly assume that on the intermediate day, when she did not perform, the ceremony took place. The significant play chosen for the occasion seems to point to something of the kind.* Yet we might have a suspicion that in the case of *mesalliance* as this, certainly Mr. Clive would not have been in such a hurry to have it so promptly proclaimed to the world; and it may be that this change of name was in consequence of the separation which speedily followed the marriage.

---

* When Mr. Charles Kean married Miss Tree, in Dublin, both played in " The Honeymoon " on the day of the marriage.

CHAPTER II.

Struggle with Mrs. Cibber for the part of " Polly."—How the Town amused itself with their contentions.—The revolt against Manager Highmore; "Kitty's" straightforward behaviour. — The praises of Fielding and others.—Separates from Mr. Clive ; visits Dublin.

ALL through her course, our actress showed herself combative and even contentious, whenever she fancied that "her rights" were encroached upon. Conscious of the scrupulous fashion in which she did her duty to the public, she claimed that the same regard should be paid to her by her employers ; and when these attempted to take advantage of her good nature, she was as spirited in resisting such encroachments as the most troublesome of her sex. We find her almost from the commencement, engaged in some conflict with managers, or else in vigorously resisting the attempt of some other performer to encroach upon her privileges. But when she came to be enlisted under the fair, firm, and equitable rule of Garrick, we hear no more of these troubles, and she settled down into the painstaking, conscientious actress, thinking only how she could best perform her duties to the public, to the theatre, and to herself.

We have spoken of the difficulty of calling up before us the particular charm and gift which has made an actor popular in his generation. But in the case of the captivating Mrs. Susannah Cibber, we can realise perfectly what a tender, sympathetic performer she was. Her letters are those of a charming unobtrusive woman, full of a gentle

raillery and subdued sorrow. The daughter of an accomplished musician, Arne, she herself possessed musical gifts
of no common order; and her eagerness to make a figure
in this department, was to bring about a serious quarrel
with so redoubtable an antagonist as Mrs. Clive. These
two eminent ladies were now to be in conflict, struggling
for the possession of a favourite character.

The extraordinary success of the "Beggar's Opera" at
Lincoln's Inn Fields, with the singular interest excited by
the sympathetic character of *Polly*, whose representative
had won the coronet of a Duchess by her performance,
made every actress long for the opportunity of distinguishing
herself in so taking a character. Mrs. Clive was "in possession" of the part at Drury Lane, but it was naturally felt
that a good voice and a piquant style, were not all the
qualities requisite for a perfect *Polly*. The whole cast of
the character is sad and touching, as will be seen from the
description given by Mr. Cambridge to Boswell. "It was
saved," he said, "on the first night by the song,

> 'O ponder well, be not severe;'

the audience being much affected by the innocent looks of
Polly when she came to these two lines,

> 'For on the rope that hangs, my dear,
> Depends poor Polly's life.'"

There could have been little of this kind of sympathy
furnished by the vivacious Kitty, who would naturally
emphasize, in her way, the more farcical portions. In
1736, unluckily, Mrs. Cibber conceived a wish to perform
Polly, and at the same time oust the actual possessor of
the part. The hubbub that followed was inconceivable;
Mrs. Clive appealed to her friends in *The Town*, Mrs.

Cibber did the same. But this ill feeling gradually developed from mere "clashing," into perfect animosity. "No two women of high rank," says Davies, "ever hated one another more unreservedly than these great Dames of the theatre. But though the passions of each were as lofty as those of the first Duchess, yet they wanted the courtly art of concealing them."

These claims of Mrs. Cibber were at a later period very unfairly pressed—and the honest Clive was often put aside to gratify her whim. Thus in March, 1755, when the comedy of "Rule a Wife," was brought out, Mrs. Cibber insisted on having the light, lively part of *Estifania*, though Mrs. Clive, "as the superior comic actress of the theatre," was really entitled to it. The manager too, wished to see her in it, though, as Davies suspected, he and Woodward secretly wished to keep her "out of it." The gay ladies of comedy, however, were surely not in her line, for she lacked the refinement and delicacies, though not the spirit, necessary to the part.

"When Mrs. Cibber was cast for *Polly*," wrote Victor to Theo. Cibber, nigh twenty years later, "she was very young, handsome, and an approved good singer. She had every requisite to make the best *Polly* that had ever appeared, and so had Mrs. Clive for *Lucy*: it would undoubtedly have been a fine entertainment so performed—but Clive was there in possession of the public voice—she was disgusted at the thought of leaving *Polly*, and lodged her complaint. What a storm was raised! but their favourite, right or wrong was to be supported, though against judgment and common sense. I remember I was one of your friends that advised you to give it up—your wife was then new to the stage, and the match was perfectly unequal, and so the only opportunity of seeing the "Beggar's Opera" in perfection was lost."

"I find," says Fielding, speaking in the character of Mrs. Cibber's husband, the little viper 'Theo,' "that by our theatrical squabbles and altercations we make as much amusement to the town in a morning as by our performance in an evening. The contentions for the part of *Polly* between Mrs. Clive and my late—I was going to say wife —but a late woman who was called by many a name.— That contest, I remark, furnished a copious topic for conversation, argument, and publication, and ended with noise and uproars in the playhouse. The consequence of all these addresses has been this : the town is called into the playhouse, as the *dernier ressort*, to judge of things." This has always been the case with that supersensitive and touchy corps, who, on the slightest assumed affront or injury, carry all their dirty linen to the market and wash it there before the amused crowd.

So ludicrous was the contention between the two angry ladies, that Woodward, then (1736) engaged at Lincoln Inn Fields, brought out an *apropos* piece on the subject, entitled :—

THE BEGGARS' PANTOMIME;
OR, THE CONTENDING COLUMBINES.

The printed version of which he dedicates to the two actresses " who had a violent contention for Polly."

Here the two columbines are seen to contend with each other for the part; and no doubt burlesqued the manner of the actresses. Thus :—

[*A Beggar enters in a hurry.*]

Beg.—Mr. Prompter, Mr. Prompter, [*enter Prompter*] What the devil is the meaning of this step; have you a design to ruin me ?

Prompt.—I assure you 'tis not my fault. Mrs. Roberts and Mrs. Hamilton are quarrelling who shall be first columbine. They scolded as long as they had breath, and now they have set themselves down to send letters to the public papers to inform them of this ill usage.

Woodward, however, apologised in his Preface for the liberty he took :—" When I publicly declare this trifling piece was meant only to promote the theatre to which I belong, I hope you will have more good nature than to imagine I designed to affront two ladies I am utterly a stranger to. Your paper was making such a bustle about the town, and its being so much the public talk of coffee houses, I thought it no bad scheme to make use of the opportunity, and introduce something like your contention on the stage. I immediately made use of the subject." He adds that the whole was written, mounted, and produced within ten days.

A ballad too, in the strain of " Chevy Chase " was also published, ridiculing the squabble :—

> Heaven prosper long our noble King,
>   Our lives, and save us all ;
> A woeful quarrel lately did
>   In Drury Lane befall.
> To charm the pit with speech and song
>   Dame Cibber took her way :
> Players may rue who are unborn
>   The quarrel of that day.
> Cibber, the syren of the stage,
>   A vow to heaven did make,
> Full twenty nights in Polly's part
>   She'd make the playhouse shake.
> When as these tidings came to Clive,
>   Fierce Amazonian dame :
> " Who is it thus," in rage she cries,
>   " Dares rob me of my claim ? "

With that she to the green room flew,
Where Cibber meek she found ;
And sure if friends had not been by,
She had fell'd her to the ground."—(Jan., 1737.)

Fielding too, in his "Historical Register," produced in
the same year, makes merry over the ladies and this contest.
One of the characters Sowrvit asks :

" Hey day ! what's become of your two *Pollys?* "

Medley.—Damned—Sir, damned ! They were damned
at my first rehearsal : for which reason I have cut them
out, and, to tell you the truth, I think the town has
honoured them enough, with talking of them for a whole
month.

Even Chetwood, her admirer, had his little fling, in the
"Dramatic Congress," 1743, where he makes Kitty give
a characteristic account of herself :—

Dash.—Good manners oblige us to enquire on ladies
first; therefore Miss Kitty, we shall be glad to know
what you have to allege against the Basha, and submit
it to yourself, whether he has not always behaved with
the strictest regard to your interests.

Kitty.—As to his regarding my interest he never did it
in particular, but when it very largely conduced to
his own. I look after the stage as a very precarious
situation. I have, by my assiduity, endeavoured to
please the town. If ever I met with any favour it was
from *them* not *him ;* . . . Did he not make use of
all the arts he was master of to depreciate me with the
audience ? Witness the contest he created about *Polly,*
when Callista and I stood the shock of the audience
alternately for several nights together. When Sylvia

E

was engaged to him he endeavoured as much to set her up as my rival, but the town would not permit it."

Dash urges in reply that the manager's motive might have been "to display the merits of the two ladies to an equal degree. He certainly increased *Kitty's* salary so extravagantly as to make it much above any woman's on the stage now."

Kitty answers, "not near so much esteem as he showed for his foreigners, who, at the weekly expense of near eighty pounds, convinced him that they were almost useless, whilst I and others at a much lower rate, contributed to the payment of them: notwithstanding which, he is about lowering the salary he previously agreed with me for, and that before he has discharged the little arrears due to me."

Dash.—Hold, madam, do you really think he could reasonably afford to give you the salary he did.

Kitty.—As you have been so free with me, I must as freely tell you that I wonder you can enter into a league with one, who, though he would be thought a gentleman, seduced several of your performers from you.

Dash.—O child, it is fair gaming.

Kitty.—Well I'll not be lowered whilst I am capable of meriting what I have had all along, and that's my resolution."

Yet in spite of the ill-will which such disputes must have engendered, when the two ladies were engaged at Drury Lane in 1747, under Garrick, we find Mrs. Cibber (on Sep. 17th) performing the coveted *Polly* with great effect, and her rival Clive taking the part of *Lucy;* which, however, must have fitted her far better. When Mrs.

Cibber was gone, she also tolerated one of her friends, Miss Edwards—afterwards Mrs. Mozeen, in the same character. Nay, before this, she was content not to figure in the piece at all, when Mrs. Pritchard took the part of *Lucy* to Mrs. Cibber's *Polly*. No better proof could be given of the complaisance of this worthy actress, whenever the interests of the theatre called for it.

We next find our heroine concerned, to some extent, in a revolt against the managers, a rather entertaining episode, in which she acquitted herself with moderation and credit. Actors are mostly a sensitive and unreflecting race, and are usually drawn into such rebellions, in consequence of some sense of fancied injury. But Mrs. Clive here was to show her usual good sense. ·

After the happy, judicious reign of Cibber and his colleagues, it was the fortune of Drury Lane Theatre to pass from one bankrupt manager to another, under whose dissipated rule the whole fell into disorder. The first of these rash adventurers was "John Highmore, Esq., of Hampton Court," a gentleman with £800 a year. Having offered by way of frolic, to play *Lothario* for one night— it was for a wager at White's Club, with Lord Limerick,—he was so transported with the applause he received and the great receipts, that he at once purchased shares in the theatre and became a manager. At this time, by a curious oversight, the players were not bound to have any agreements or "articles," and they could leave almost without notice. In his company was that truly detestable being, Theo. Cibber, who seems to have been a bad son, a bad husband, a bad actor,—who was always plotting some intrigue, and finally lost in a storm, sailing to Ireland with a whole cargo of properties, to say nothing of "Madox, the great wire-rope dancer." Before Highmore had been in office a fortnight, Theo. had spirited up a revolt against the manager : and, though his own father had just been paid £3,000 for his share, the son did his best to get possession of the theatre, and drive out the managers. There were probably real grievances to complain of, but nothing to warrant such a rebellion. The principal players all joined him, such as old Mills, Johnson, Miller, Griffin, Harper, and Mrs. Heron. But we find that Mrs. Clive and Mrs. Horton, though they were dissatisfied, disdained to join in the revolt, and held by their master. The fact that two women—Mrs. Wilks, the widow of her old theatrical idol, and Mrs. Booth—were in the direction, may have contributed to this loyalty :—of which, Fielding expressed his admiration in the warmest terms.

'The part," he says,* "you have maintained in the present dispute between the players and patentees of 1733, is so full of honour, that had it been in higher life, it would have given you the reputation of the greatest heroine of the age. You looked on the cases of Mr. Highmore and Mr. Wilks with compassion, nor could any promises or views of interest sway you to desert them : nor have you scrupled any fatigue (particularly the part which at so short a warning you undertook in this farce) to support the cause of those you imagined injured, and for this you have been so far from endeavouring to exact an exorbitant reward from persons little able to afford it, that I have known you offer to act for nothing, rather than the patentees should be injured by the dissensions of the audience."

---

* Preface to "The Intriguing Chambermaid," 1734.

There is something hearty in this testimony, which furnishes an admirable idea of the sterling, upright character of this woman. "In short, if honour, good gratitude, and good sense, joined with the most entertaining humour, are titles to public esteem, I think you may be sure of it." In this we have homage to her behaviour in a particular transaction—a warm and most genuine encomium'; we feel that here is a thoroughly "good creature," spirited and ready to sacrifice her interest to her feelings. And he goes on : "But great a favourite as you are at present with the audience, you would be much more were they acquainted with your private character; could they see you laying out a great part of the profits which arise to you for entertaining them so well, *in support of an aged father ; did they see you, who can charm them on the stage with personating the foolish and vicious characters of your sex, acting in real life the part of the best wife, the best daughter, the best sister, and the best friend.*"

This is really an extraordinary testimony, and there is something exceedingly welcome in the portrait. The old Raftor supported by his promising daughter, with his broken family, is pleasant to think of. Thus we find her interesting character gradually filling in. It might almost be added, that she was a good sister too, for we find her brother at the same theatre, where she had, no doubt, got him engaged, and coupled with her in benefits, which he was certainly otherwise not entitled to. He did not emerge at all, and made no figure in his profession.

At the praise of " a good wife " the experienced theatrical reader may be inclined to pause and perhaps shake his head; for shortly after these encomiums were uttered, she and her husband separated. Of the incident and its causes nothing is known, but they never came together again. Victor, who knew her well, hints that the fault was not hers, nor is it likely that it was; though it may be that her independent nature and temper would resent any presumed superiority on the ground of station. A blunt, sturdy woman, warm tempered also, would be unduly sensitive on so delicate a point, and perhaps scornful in reference to Mr. Clive's good family and "Baron Clive." We have only a single glimpse of this obscure gentleman, furnished by Taylor, the journalist :—

"He was," he says, "a very learned and intelligent man, by all accounts : but without practice in his profession; he was therefore invited to become the domestic companion of Mr. Ince, a gentleman of fortune, and reputed to be the Templar in the club of the *Spectator*. Mr. Ince was well known to be a frequent contributor to that admirable periodical work. My old friend, the Rev. Richard Penneck of the British Museum, knew Mr. Ince, and told me that he retained the practice, as mentioned in the *Spectator*, of visiting the playhouse almost every evening, as long as his health and age would admit."

This acceptance of the post of "gentleman companion" —shows him to have been rather "a poorish creature"— as Carlyle phrases it—and his vivacious lady may have reproached him with a similar tendency to live upon her earnings. This however, is all matter of speculation.

While the seceders retired to the Haymarket, the deserted manager took some violent steps to force them back to their duty. Such was the historic case of the arrest of Harper, the player, &c. All ended in the return of the prodigals— who, it seems in point of law, actually had a claim to possession of the lease of the theatre, though not to the patent, and it was so decided by the Court of King's Bench, on Nov. 12, 1733, upon an ejectment. Highmore however held the patent, without which they could do nothing, but the struggle and the cost of legal proceedings utterly ruined him. This "added to his constantly failing audiences was sufficient to destroy a much larger estate than his: and it was with the utmost difficulty he held out through the season. He was a man of humanity and strict honour: many instances fatally proved that his word, solemnly given—which was his custom—was sufficient for the performance, though ever so injurious to himself."

This in itself was a recommendation to our actress, and accounts for her loyalty through the crisis. "As the season," goes on Victor, "was advanced, he was reduced to the necessity of beating his drum for volunteers—several recruits offered from strolling companies, but I remember none, of any promise, but Macklin. In this maimed condition the business, of course, went tamely on." Poor Clive!

During the season of 1743, and thus early in her career, the impetuous spirit of the actress broke out on the score of some grievance in the distribution of parts in Fielding's "Wedding Day." The author could thus good-naturedly exhibit her peculiarities—in some pleasant lines,—from which it will be seen that our actress when roused, would express her displeasure in good round oaths :—

> " Where is this scoundrel poet ?
> Fine work indeed ! By —— the town shall know it."
> Fielding, who heard, and saw her passion rise,
> Thus answered calmly :—" Prithee, Clive, be wise,
> The part will suit your humour, taste, and size."
> " Ye·lie ! ye lie ! ungrateful as thou art,
> My matchless talents claim the lady's part ;
> And all who judge, by J—— C——, agree,
> None ever played the gay coquette like me."
> Thus said and swore the celebrated Noll."

Dublin was at this time a great nursery for the stage, and theatrical entertainments were in high vogue. It had two flourishing theatres and good companies, and the managers were always eager to engage new and rising talent. It was in the year 1741, when Garrick was to make the town " horn mad," that she accepted an engagement to go thither with Quin, Ryan, and a dancer—Madame Chateneuf. They appeared at the theatre in Aungier Street, and the season commenced with " a brilliancy never before known in Irish annals." She was " welcomed with the most uncommon civilities, and received the greatest advantages," which she acknowledged afterwards in the warmest and most grateful terms.*

" Mr. Quin opened in his favourite part of *Cato*, to as crowded an audience as the theatre could contain. Mrs. Clive next appeared as *Lappet* in "The Miser;" she certainly was one of the best that ever played it; and Mr. Ryan came forward in *Iago* to Mr. Quin's *Othello*. With such excellent performers, we may naturally suppose the plays were admirably sustained. Perhaps it will scarcely be credited that so finished a comic actress as Mrs. Clive could so far mistake her abilities as to play *Lady Townly* to Mr. Quin's *Lord Townly*, and Mr. Ryan's *Manly*, *Cordelia* to Mr. Quin's *Lear* and Mr. Ryan's *Edgar*, &c. However, she made ample amends by her performance of *Nell*, "The Virgin Unmasked," " The Country Wife," and *Euphrosyne* in " Comus," which was got up on purpose and acted for the first time in this kingdom.

---

* The Dublin folk have always been particularly cordial in welcoming players—even the wretched Mrs. Sumbel, who had a beautiful face.

"The "Masque of Comus," though one of the most beautiful pieces of poetry in our language, yet requires to be
uncommonly supported to render it pleasing to an English
audience.   But in this instance it was indeed a treat to the
judicious.   Mr. Quin spoke *Comus*; the *Elder Brother* was
played by Mr. Ryan; Mrs. Clive, *Euphrosyne*, and the
other characters were disposed of with great care and pro-
priety.   The celebrated Mr. Dubourg prepared the music,
Pasquilino led the band, and the dances were executed by
Monsieur Laluze, Mademoiselle Chateneuf, and others. This
was allowed to be the best entertainment presented to the
public for many years, and during the short time they had
to stay, was repeated three times.   As soon as Aungier
street theatre closed, Mr. Ryan and Mrs. Clive returned to
London."

F

CHAPTER III.

*Revolt against Fleetwood, headed by Garrick.—Mrs. Clive
joins the Deserters.—Her "appeal to the Town."*

ON her return she found the whole theatrical community
in confusion. The manager of Drury Lane, having ex-
hausted all his resources, both of money and chicanery, had
been forced to withdraw, and utterly broken und bankrupt,
retired abroad, where he died in distress. A gay and
wealthy gentleman named Fleetwood now came in, only
twenty-one years old and enjoying £6000 a year. He was
described as being "agreeable in his person, and the qualities
of his mind and amiableness of his disposition carried with
them invincible attractions. He was affable and engaging
in his address, which was the last and only remaining good
quality he had kept with him till his death; and no doubt
that would have vanished with the rest if he had not found
it *of constant use to him in his business with the world.*"
This neatly sarcastic touch came from Victor, a stage
manager, whom we have been quoting. It was unfortunate
for Mrs. Clive that she, after her sacrifices, found herself under the direction of another spendthrift, "though,
I am informed he came a ruined man into the management,
and that he was for some years a gainer by his purchase
gambling." The rough Macklin acted as his deputy and
dealt with the performers, who were ground down, left
with salaries unpaid, while mortgagees and bailiffs held
the place. A money lender named Pierson was the virtual
controller of the theatre. He was favoured however by
one happy stroke which might have done for him what

the engagement of the obscure "Kean, from Dorchester," did for the broken Drury Lane Committee. Meanwhile his management staggered on.

The sudden rising of the star of GARRICK, in this general gloom, is a story too well known to be more than alluded to here. He was fortunate in possessing that rare combination of administrative power—analogous to that of some great political minister in leading the House of Commons—with extraordinary histrionic ability—a happy union which is found in the most prominent actor of our day. The effect of two such powerful forces in a single person becomes almost irresistible. The new actor had taken service with Fleetwood, and had continued with him for about a year; but his sagacious eye soon saw that he was wasting his powers in such a position. Still he enjoyed what was then considered an enormous salary as will be seen from the Drury Lane List for the season of 1742-43.*

The total salary list was computed at about £4,000. The amount is of course calculated in the number of *acting weeks*, which seem to have been about thirty-five in the year. The treasurer added that in this account, "no computation was made of gold tickets, which are sometimes very considerable." These "gold tickets" were presents to

---

* Mr. Garrick, £630; with two clear benefits (one paying £50), £500; total, £1130. Macklin, at 9 guineas per week, and 6 guineas for his wife, £525; with a clear benefit (paying £50 to the house), £230; total, £755. Mrs. Woffington, at 7 guineas a week, £364; and a clear benefit—say, £130; clothes, £50; total, £644. Mrs. Pritchard, at £7 10s. certain, £250; clear benefit, £180; clothes, £50; total, £480. Mrs. CLIVE, £15 15s. certain, £525; clear benefit, £200; clothes, £50; tickets at her benefit, as per agent, £21; total, £796.

the amount of ten or twenty pounds, made by patrons or admirers on the occasion of a benefit.

With so handsome a salary, and a leading position at the first metropolitan theatre, it is likely that Garrick would have been contented. But he found it impossible to obtain his money; and he, with the other players, was disgusted at the introduction of vulgar shows; for " monsters " were hired from Sadler's Wells and the fairs, with rope dancers and tumblers. His salary at last was some six hundred pounds in arrears. Here the worm turned. In May, 1743, he positively declined to act, and absented himself for three weeks. Finding this step of no use, he planned the well-known " revolt."

What must have more immediately led to this step, was a rumour or a suspicion that the patentees had entered into a secret agreement or " cartel," to deal with the players in common ; so that if a deserter applied to the other house, he was not to receive any increase of salary, or at least should only obtain what the managers had agreed to give. This put the players at their mercy, as there were only two houses to give them employment. Garrick's plan, as he unfolded it, was that they should all desert and set up for themselves; and he had been encouraged to believe that he could obtain a license from the Duke of Grafton to open the Opera House. Macklin, who was more or less *liéd* with the manager, suggested going to him first and announcing their purpose, which might bring him to terms ; but Garrick was against this course. About a dozen of the leading performers joined in the revolt, including Havard, Barry, Mills, Macklin, Mrs. Pritchard, and Mrs. Clive. Application was made at once to the Duke of Grafton, who refused to grant the license. Fleetwood speedily filled up his thinned

ranks with recruits from country companies. The prudent
Garrick, seeing that the scheme had failed, at once opened
negotiations for reconciliation with the manager, for himself
and his friends. He was favourably received, and was
promised restoration ; a few of the others were not taken
back ; but Fleetwood could now pick and choose. Macklin,
whose conduct he considered treacherous in the extreme,
was proscribed. This actor was furious with Garrick, whom
he accused of betraying him and his friends, and he insisted
that in honour and also by the terms of their signed agreement, he was bound to sink or swim with the rest—that all
should be restored or all stand out. Garrick admitted this
strict interpretation of the bond, but urged the reasonable
view, that it was unfair that all the actors should starve for
his sake. It was a matter clearly of compromise and in-
demnification, and he handsomely offered to pay him out of
his own pocket six pounds a week, and secure from the
manager an engagement at three pounds a week for Mrs.
Macklin. But Macklin was a determined, rather turbu-
lent being, with much of his countrymen's vindictiveness
in dealing with injuries real or supposed. He would hear
of nothing but the bond, and assailed Garrick in pamphlets
in which the mildest phrases were, "your treachery," "you
have no notion of honour," &c. To which the other replied,
tout bonnement, that "it was a falsehood." It ended by most
of the revolted players being restored, though at lower
salaries ; but the wrong-headed Macklin was cast out. But
there was to be another scapegoat—the intrepid Clive. She
had indeed joined the revolt at its early stage, for she could
never brook ill-treatment ; and it is characteristic that she
should have chosen to stand by the poor, cheated players
who had been cast off by the principals. We can see at

once that her good nature was touched by the piteous appeal those unhappy victims now addressed to Garrick, now to Macklin, imploring them not to stand upon these punctilios, but to arrange matters for them, or their families would certainly' starve. Our actress declined to follow Mr. Garrick in his comfortable compromise, though not unwilling to accept an engagement from the manager on her old terms.

For this natural proceeding she was pursued with much obloquy and abusive gossip, until she was at last driven to lay her story before the town and vindicate her behaviour. To this mode of appeal she was rather too much addicted, from a wish to stand well with her patrons. There accordingly appeared

The Case of Mrs. Clive

Submitted to the Public,

a diminutive little pamphlet. It is well known that Kitty was deficient, not only in style, but even in spelling : so it is not unlikely that she was aided in this venture by Fielding or some literary friend ; but the language is unmistakably hers, and there is one passage rather "Irish and less nice," which comes perilously near to being "a bull."*

She began by saying bluntly, that the reason for her not acting that season was the advice of her friends. "Such appeals as the present," she went on to say, "were by some thought presuming and pertinent, but where injustice and oppression were concerned—this could never be a matter of indifference to the public—she appeals without affectation to her own claims on her regard of that public."

---

*This little *brochure* is in the Museum, and is likely enough to be unique. I have not seen another, nor even the advertisement of another, in any catalogue.

"I am the more encouraged to hope this from experience : it having been observed that those performers, who have had the happiness to please on the stage, and who never did anything to offend the public, when they have been injured by those who presided over theatres, have seldom, if ever, failed of redress upon representing the hardships they met with. If any think I treat this matter too seriously, I hope they will remember that however trifling such things may appear to them, to me, who am so much concerned in them, they are of great importance, such as my liberty and livelihood depend on."

She then proceeds to explain the condition of the actors in reference to the managers. "They were quite helpless, as only two theatres were authorised, and the managers, connected together, complained of the actors' salaries being too great, and accordingly a false account was published of them in the daily paper, by whom I will not say. Whether or no some particular salaries were so, I will not pretend to determine. But whether the expense of the theatre was too high or otherwise, it was not the refusal of the actors to submit to a reduction that drove them to secede, but the tyranny of the two managers." She then dwelt on her own particular hardship. When the revolters were obliged to return to their duty, she was offered by the manager of Drury Lane such terms as bore no proportion to what he gave other performers, or to those he had offered her at the beginning of the season. These she accordingly refused, and she applied to the other theatre,—"for I knew it had been settled by some sort of agreement that part of the actors were to go to Covent Garden, and others to Drury Lane." Yet though Covent Garden had before tempted her with high offers, and offered exactly the same terms she had found at Drury Lane, she was, however, persuaded to accept "some very little better," and had to submit to paying a sum of money for her benefit, though she had enjoyed one clear of all expense for nine years before.

" When I was fixed at this theatre, I determined to stay there ; I did in all things which related to my profession, submit entirely to the manager's direction, and with the help of other principal performers, did greatly promote his interest, as was evident from the audiences, after we went to act there ; but I found by his behaviour, it was designed I should not continue with him, but return the next season to Drury Lane.

" The agreements betwixt that manager and me were verbal, but made before two gentlemen of character and fortune, on whom I must depend for the fulfilling of them : they were for one year. At the end of the acting season, the manager sent an office keeper to me with some salary that was due, who required a receipt in full. I told him a very great part of my agreement was yet due, and requested to see the manager, who came and acknowledged them, and promised to bring one of the gentlemen who was present at our engagements in a day or two and pay me ; but he has not paid me," adds Kitty in her downright style, "nor have I ever seen him since, or as much as heard from him."

" It has always been a custom in theatres, that if any actor or actress was to be discharged, or their allowance lessened, they were acquainted with it at the end of the season : the reason of this will appear to be the giving them a proper notice to provide for themselves.· This the manager of Covent Garden did to all his company whom he designed to discharge, or whose allowance was to be

lessened, *except to me*, which made me actually then conclude he determined I should continue with him, till I was
undeceived by his play bills with the names of other
actresses in parts I used to perform. So that he has not
only broke through the customs of the theatre, but those
in practice almost everywhere, in dismissing me, and has
done me a real injury in such an unprecedented act of
injustice. For had I been informed of this design at the
end of the season, I could have made terms to have acted
in *Ireland*, where I had met with most uncommon civilities,
and received very great advantages, which I shall ever
remember with the utmost gratitude, and take this and
every other opportunity to acknowledge.

*　*　*　*　*　*　*

" It is pretended by the management that they have the
same right to discharge an actor that a master has to turn
away a servant, than which nothing can be more false and
absurd: for when a master dismisses a servant there are
many thousands besides to apply to, but when managers
dismiss an actor, where are they to apply to? It is unlaw-
ful to act anywhere but with them. Necessity or inclination
brings every one to the stage : if the former happens to be
the case, they will not readily find an employment, and if
the latter they will not be fit for one, so that it will appear
an act of great injustice and oppression. . . . . But
there is a very melancholy instance that the actor's
demands is not the reason of dismissing them, but the will
of the manager alone. Since last season an actor and
actress returned to Drury Lane, under such abatements as
that manager thought proper, and such as were in no
degree equal to their merit : and yet at the beginning of the
season were dismissed after having been from their infancy

G

on the stage and having no other profession to live by, and very numerous families to support.

"The manager of Drury Lane, though he can't but know I am disengaged from the other theatre, has not made any application to me to act with him, which he has done to several others who quitted that stage at the time I did. The reasons which obliged me to leave him still subsist. He owes me a hundred and fifty pounds, twelve shillings, which he acknowledged to be justly due, and promised payment of it by last Christmas to a person of too great consequence to mention here, the greater part of it (which?) money I expended for clothes for his use. He offered me last season, not near half as much as he afterwards agreed to give another performer, and less than he gave to some others in his company, so that I must conclude that there is a design to distress me, and reduce me to such terms as I cannot comply with.

"I am sorry I am reduced to say anything in favour of myself : but I think I merit as much as another performer, and the managers are so desirous to convince me of the contrary, I hope I shall be excused, especially when I declare that at this time, I am not in the least vain of my profession.

"As to my performances, the audiences are the only and proper judges : but I may *venture to affirm that my labour and application have been greater than any other performer on the stage.* I have not only acted in almost all the plays, but in farces and musical entertainments ; and very frequently two parts in a night, even to the prejudice of my health. I have been at great expense in masters for singing : for which article alone the managers give five and six pounds a week. My additional expenses in belonging to the theatre amount to upwards of one hundred pounds a year in clothes and other necessaries; and the pretended great salaries of ten and twelve pounds a week, which have been so artfully and falsely represented to the town, to the prejudice of the actors, will, upon enquiry, appear to be no more than half as much; since they performed last season, at the theatres, very seldom above three or four days a week.

"I have now finished all I proposed: I have shown in how aggravating a manner, without any reason assigned, I have been turned out of Covent Garden Theatre. The manager of Drury Lane, though he cannot but know what just reasons I had for quitting him, has never applied to me to return, nor made the least excuse for not paying my arrears.

"The reason of my taking the liberty to communicate these things to the public is most earnestly to intercede for their favour and protection, from whom I have always met with great generosity and indulgence. For, as I have always declared in a letter published by me last year in the daily papers, that I had not a fortune to support me independent of my profession. I doubt not, but it will appear I have made any considerable acquisition to it since, having not received two hundred pounds salary for acting in plays, farces, and singing: though other performers have received more than twice that sum. I have in consideration of these hardships been promised the protection of many ladies to whom I have the honour to be personally known, and will not doubt the concurrence of a public in receiving my performance in the best manner I am, at present, capable of, which I shall always gratefully acknowledge."—C. CLIVE.

Such was this pleasant and effective appeal—in which we seem to hear the actual tones of the sturdy actress.

This scene of confusion was made worse confounded by broils between the actors as well as between the rival houses. During the rebellion Mrs. Cibber proposed to give a benefit for the purpose of raising soldiers, which the manager of Drury Lane received with some disgust. But it caused an uproar in the green-room. "I was cursed," she says, "with all the elegance of phrase that reigns behind the scenes; and Mrs. Clive swore she would not play the part of *Lucy*." She accordingly transferred the. scheme to the other house, where it was accepted and carried out with great spirit. There was certainly no love lost between these two ladies.

During the interval we find her appearing at the Haymarket Opera House, on the occasion of a "Concert of Vocal and Instrument Musick" given under the distinguished patronage of the Prince and Princess of Wales. Here she sang in company with Mr. Lowe and Miss Edwards. Her first appearance at Covent Garden was on December 7th, 1743, when she performed *Lappet* in "The Miser," one of the usual chambermaids: with *Ophelia* on the 14th, followed by *Nell*, *Polly*, and other favourite characters.

At the various Fairs held in London at Bartholomew and Southwark, it was the practise for some leading players to open Booths, and perform popular plays. Mr. Fielding was one of these *entrepreneurs*,—indeed we find him performing himself. Here Mrs. Clive figured. "At the Booth of Fawkes Pinchbeck will be performed 'Britons, Strike Home;' *Don Superbo Hispaniola Pistole* by Mrs. Cibber; *Donna Americana* by Mrs. Clive, *The Favourite of the Town*."

CHAPTER IV.

Mrs. Clive engaged by Garrick. — Her Style of Acting described.—Disappearance of " the chambermaid " as a character.— Breadth of Acting.— Her Quarrels with " Peg " Woffington. — " Scenes " between the ladies described.— Quarrels with Woodward — with Garrick —amantium iræ.

W HEN Garrick, in 1747, made his first venture as manager, thus taking the inevitable step to which every popular and engrossing actor is led, he gathered about him a strong and judiciously selected company. These by his admirable training and firm rule, he moulded into an admirable company, whose effect on the English stage has been remarkable, suggesting the influence of the great Comédie Française in this country. In his corps were found Mrs. Cibber, Mrs. Pritchard, Macklin, Barry, Mrs. Woffington, and—to add brightness to the composition—the vivacious Mrs. Clive as " leading comick" (the old quaint phrase) or "singing chambermaid."

Being thus fixed in a well-regulated flourishing company, our actress fell into the ranks, performing a round of important characters, maturing her powers from practice, and, in Johnson's phrase, " increasing the public stock of harmless pleasure." In a company of such a kind the opportunities for developing histrionic power are boundless ; for the " stock " pieces brought forward at regular intervals belong to fixed " castes," and each character belongs to one regular performer. His or her special gifts become associated in the mind of the public with the particular part,—the appearance, the tones, and manner, are curiously associated with it, — while a new performer appears strange and unfamiliar. It will be remembered how the late Mr. Phelps became thus so bound-up, as it were, with the vigorous eccentricities of *Sir Pertinax*, as to make it almost impossible for another player to discharge the part. He *was*, in every point, the old gnarled, cantankerous Scotch Baronet. It is astonishing in these times to find what a number of characters were thus undertaken by a well-established performer during the course of a long career. We find that Munden had a "list" that reached to over two hundred: Mrs. Clive's included nearly the same. But of these there are only a few in which she excelled, and which were regularly called for, and these did not exceed a dozen. There was *Nell* in "The Devil to Pay;" *Flora*, the waiting maid, in "The Wonder," which, it was declared, she made almost as important as the leading character; *Lady Bab*, in the amusing "High Life below Stairs;" *Catherine*, in "Catherine and Petruchio;" the vulgar *Mrs. Heidleberg*, in "The Clandestine Marriage."

It is now difficult to form any idea of the great powers with which she held her audiences. There is no actress now on the stage of her peculiar *genre*—the type is lost: for the reason, we may presume, that the type of the vivacious, bustling, obstreperous lady has disappeared from the ranks of society. The course of manners would appear to have abolished *high* spirits as indecorous. Mrs. Jordan would seem to have been the last of the Irish, or hoydenish players. Davies, who had seen her often, and who had powers of critical analysis, tells us that "many dramatic pieces are now lost to the stage, for want of her animating

spirit to preserve them"—a judicious remark of wide
meaning. It explains why revivals of old comedies in our
time fall so "flat." The actors, unfamiliar with many-
shaded characters, have not the skill to interpret or fill
them in. The performance has as bald and barren a result
as the reading of the piece in "the closet,"—a dreary pro-
cess—save in the case of Congreve's comedies. This was
proved during a recent revival of "The Clandestine
Marriage," which was listened to with curiosity rather than
interest; and all might wonder how Mrs. Clive could have
"made anything" of so poor a part as *Mrs. Heidleberg.*
He goes on:—"A more extensive walk in comedy than
hers cannot be imagined; the Chambermaid in every varied
shape which art or nature could lend her; characters of
caprice and affectation, from the high-bred *Lady Fanciful,*
to the vulgar *Mrs. Heidleberg*; country girls, romps,
hoydens and dowdies, superannuated beauties, viragos and
humourists. To a strong and melodious voice, with an ear
for music, she added all the sprightly action requisite."
Strong mimicry was also one of her gifts. "She had an
inimitable talent in ridiculing the extravagant actions,
impertinent consequence, and insignificant parade of the
female opera singers. Her mirth was so genuine, that
whether it was restrained to the arch sneer, and the suppressed half laugh—widened to the broad grin, or extended
to the downright honest burst of loud laughter,—her
audience was sure to accompany her."

These graphic touches bring her vividly before us.
Fielding was no less judicious in his praise. "Mrs. Clive
is esteemed by all an excellent comic actress; and as she
has a prodigious fund of natural spirit and humour off the
stage, she makes the most of the poet's on it. Nothing,

though ever so barren, even though it exceeds the limits of nature, can be flat in her hands. She heightens all characters of humour she attempts; nor is she confined only to the hoyden Miss or pert chambermaid, but in spiritous gay characters of high life, she always appears with such air, mien, and action, as speak the gay, lively, and desirable. She has been, by persons who remember both, compared to Mrs. Mountford; and by their natural talents for the stage, I am apt to believe the comparison not unjust. I must however observe, Mrs. Mountford appeared with great success, *en Cavalier*, and made an adroit pretty fellow; Mrs. Clive does not appear in these characters, the concealing petticoat better suiting with her turn of make than the breeches. It is not from want of spirit or judgment to hit off the fop or the coxcomb, as she has evidently proved in the ballad she sings, called "The Life of a Beau," in which her action and gesture is as pleasing as in any part she performs. I could wish she would never attempt serious characters in comedy, and resign the part of *Ophelia* in ' Hamlet,' in which she is very unequal to herself. Yet all will allow, that ' take her all in all,' she has such talents as make her an excellent actress."

"If ever there were a true comic genius," breaks out the enthusiastic Victor, "Mrs. Clive is one! She, perhaps, never was equalled in her walk (as the stage term is) we are convinced, never excelled! She was always inimitable whenever she appeared in strong mark'd characters of middle, or low life—her *Nell* in "The Devil to Pay" was nature itself !—and the spirit, roguery, and speaking looks of her chambermaids, accompanied with the most expressive voice that ever satisfied the ears of an audience, has made her loss irreparable !"

"As strong humour is the great characteristic mark of an English comedy, so was it of this laughter-loving, joy-exciting actress!—her extraordinary talents could even raise a dramatic trifle, provided there was nature in it, to a character of importance—witness the *Fine Lady* in "Lethe," and the yet smaller part of *Lady Fuz*, in "The Peep behind the Curtain"—such sketches in her hands became high finished pictures!—But, that I may not be thought too partial to this favourite comedian, I will venture to assert, she could not reach the higher characters in comedy, though she was ever excellent in the affectation of them. When the high-life polish of elegance was to appear in all the conscious superiority of a *Lady Townly*, I cannot say that Mrs. Clive would have done justice to herself, or the character. To show the great power of the actress in question—I shall give an instance of it, where she forced the whole town to follow, and applaud her in a character, which she certainly did not perform as the author intended it—but which could not be resisted, and gave high entertainment to those critics, who frankly acknowledged, they were misled by the talents of the actress.—The part I mean is *Portia* in "The Merchant of Venice."—In the first place—blank verse—as it wants the truth and elegance of nature, was not uttered by Mrs. Clive with that delightful spirit which she always gave to prose ; the Lawyer's scene of *Portia* (as it is called) in the fourth act, was certainly meant by Shakespeare, to be solemn, pathetic, and affecting—the circumstances must make it so—and therefore the comic finishing which Mrs. Clive gave to the different parts of the pleadings (though greatly comic) was not in character."

H

"If therefore this theatrical genius was able to entertain, contrary to the intention of the author—what must we say of her, or what words can describe her merits, when she appeared in the fulness of her powers, and was the very person she represented?"

From this we see what a special force and attraction was in the old acting, viz., that of imparting "breadth" to the performance. This idea of "breadth" is now almost lost, and there is hardly a single performer who has the secret, or to whom it is intelligible. Yet it is the most delightful and effective of all histrionic gifts. It needs no exertion, and comes of a large, thorough view, taken of the character, in contrast to the laborious, or "niggling" (as it may be called) treatment now in fashion. An actor of "breadth," will convulse a house without moving a muscle, and will make a single, colourless sentence as significant as a whole dialogue. His eye, voice, manner, walk, all combine. Such a power had the late inimitable Buckstone during his reign. Then the public looked to him to furnish them with recreation, and with the recollection of it. As the hour of half-price drew on, the old Haymarket filled ; and about half-past ten, the farce which was to charge the air with Buckstonian humours, commenced. As the familiar twang of his voice was heard behind the scenes, a chuckle of delight passed over the house; and when he entered, brimming over with grotesque fun, a roar greeted him. " His voice," says a contemporary, " is in perfect keeping with his person : it suggests distillation ; it seems to lazily flow from a mind charged with fat thoughts and unctuous conceits. He has the true low-comedy air in his walk and gesture ; his face looks dry and red with long roasting before the footlights. He is the son of Mirth and Vulgarity. His mind is a machine which manufactures afresh the stuff it is fed on ; what is wholesome and plain is reproduced in a new form, with a different colouring and an original aroma. The downright speaking of the old dramatists can never offend or shock when spoken by refined lips ; but to such downright speaking Mr. Buckstone takes care to impart a meaning of his own, and makes plain speech a sort of intellectual perspective."

Such plenteous vivacity and absorption of the whole stage seems to have been one of our actress' most potent charms. In all the commendations of the gifts of this buoyant woman, who may be truly said to have "increased the gaiety" of the nation—we find that she was particularly extolled for one line of character, and that it was in the "*Chambermaid*" she excelled. This a generic class— the original type of which is now completely lost. In our own society the waiting maid has little to distinguish her from other servants, and little interest is taken in her—but in the old days of intrigue, the chambermaid, or rather, the confidential "ladies' maid," was a marked personage—who from her position had to be gifted with cleverness, versatility, skill, readiness of tongue, and a goodly portion of deceit. She was in the service it might be of a young heiress, followed by many suitors, and watched over by angry and zealous guardians : or of some dazzling beauty pursued by careless rakes. Here were also rivals contending with each other: so that the ." chambermaid " was the intermediary, and in fact mistress of the situation. No well conceived comedy was complete .without its saucy, amusing "chambermaid," though the character had become well worn out by the time of Sheridan, who in "The Rivals" presents a very "mild" and inefficient specimen. This suggests how curiously marked types have become lost owing to the general smoothing away of all social peculiarities—and such grotesque but amusing figures as we find in the comedies of Reynolds and Morton, would now be received with incredulity, for the reason that the originals are unfamiliar to us. The amusement furnished by the stage has certainly been impaired in consequence.

In this histrionic home she was destined to remain for twenty-two years without a break. Other performers grew touchy and techy, deserted on some affront or grievance, often to return again. She never "budged"—once she had enlisted, she stayed honourably by her colours ; her talents ripening with practise, and growing more popular every year. For the public is rarely inconstant, and relishes and respects constancy in its favourite. At the same time —like many a servant long in place—she was often troublesome to her masters and to her fellows ; and her sharp tongue on the slightest grievance or fancied oppression, was to make itself felt. Many a *mauvais quart d'heure* was she to cause the indulgent Garrick. As Tate Wilkinson said, "she knew every sore place in that sensitive being, and could make his withers wince whenever she pleased." To her companions, when they incurred her displeasure or dislike, she could make herself no less disagreeable.

Among the ladies thus enrolled, was the tragedy queen, Woffington, the well known "Peg," of whom the stage historians are fond of drawing such flattering pictures. She was in truth an interesting, good-natured, gifted creature, full of a hearty Irish good nature—impulsive and sometimes generous. Her wayward extravagant course was redeemed by her singular and scrupulous devotion to

her duty, attested by prompters and managers—the best
witnesses. She often played six nights in one week, and
"never was known to have chose occasional illnesses, which
I have seen assumed by capital performers, to the great
vexation and loss of the manager.".—Thus Mr. Hitch-
cock of the Dublin Theatre. "She never," says another,
"disappointed one audience in three winters, either by real
or assumed illness; yet I have often seen her on the stage
when she ought to have been in bed." "To her honour,"
add a third, "be it ever remembered, that while thus in
the zenith of her glory, courted and caressed by all ranks
and degrees, she made no alteration in her behaviour; she
remained the same gay, affable, obliging, good-natured
Woffington to every one around her. Not to the lowest
performer in the theatre did she refuse playing for,—out of
twenty-six benefits she acted in twenty-four." At the
same time, she could be coarse and violent, and her
squabbles and contests with other great ladies of the green-
room, were as amusing as they were notorious.

Between her and Mrs. Clive, there was a general temper
of hostility which gradually developed. Woffington had
soon found her situation with the manager uncomfortable,
and when he married—it was said that he had given her
a promise of marriage—she could not face her rather
mortifying position, and joined the rival theatre. In the
green-room Woffington reigned supreme. There she gave
way to her obstreperous spirits and boisterous humour.
When the Duchess of Queenberry was one night introduced to the green-room, the first sight that presented
itself, was Mrs. Woffington with a pot of porter in her
hand, crying out—"Confusion to all order!" "The lowest
canaille of a theatre surrounded a table covered with

mutton pies, and seemed by their manner and appearance
to realise the sentiment just toasted by the beautiful
heroine." The visitor was horrified, and rushed away
asking—"Is hell broke loose?" This grotesque picture
brings the actress vividly before us. Yet with this reckless humour there was in her a strain of sentiment and
seriousness,—a combination often found on the stage.
Anticipating a little by a few years, we find ourselves
present at another exhibition in the green-room, when an
unseemly quarrel occurred between Mrs. Clive and Mrs.
Woffington, which amused and astonished "the town."

"In the year 1754, when Henry IV. was acted, a very
beautiful and accomplished actress (Woffington) condescended, in order to give strength to the play, to act the
trifling character of *Lady Percy*. The house was far from
crowded and a celebrated comic actress (Mrs. Clive)
triumphed in the barrenness of the pit and boxes: she
threw out some expressions against the consequence of
Lady Percy. This produced a very cool and cutting
answer from the other, who reminded the former of her
playing to a much thinner audience, one of her favourite
parts, and now the ladies, not being able to restrain themselves within the bounds of cool conversation, a most
terrible fray ensued: I do not believe they went so far as
pulling of caps, but their altercation would not have dis-
graced the females of Billingsgate. While the two great
actresses were thus entertaining each other in one part of
the green-room, the admirer of Lady Percy, an old gentleman
who afterwards bequeathed her a considerable fortune, and
the brother of this comic lady (Raftor) were more seriously
employed. Mr. Swiney struck the other with his cane:
thus provoked he *very calmly laid hold of the old man's*

jaw. "Let go my jaw you villain" and "throw down your cane! Sir!" were repeatedly echoed by the combatants." Barry, who was afraid lest the audience should hear full as much of the quarrel as of the play, rushed into the room and put an end to the battle.   It is characteristic that the whole quartet were Irish.— There was published a caricature of the incident, entitled "The Green Room Scuffle." It is Davies, who, not without humour, reports the incident.   Swiney, Swinney, or Mac. Swiney, was an old dangler about the theatres, and had been a manager himself, though ever pursued by ill luck.

The same chronicler, who is always agreeable, tells us, that, even before their engagement at the same theatre, the two ladies "had clashed on various occasions, which brought forth squabbles diverting enough to their several partisans among the actors.   Woffington was well bred, seemingly very calm, and at all times mistress of herself. Clive was frank, open, and impetuous : what came uppermost in her mind she spoke without reserve : the other blunted the sharp speeches of Clive by her apparently civil but keen and sarcastic replies : thus she often threw Clive off her guard by an arch severity which the warmth of the other could not easily parry."

Mrs. Clive was present on the disastrous night of the Chinese Festival Riot, when Drury Lane Theatre was all but wrecked.   The Bill is interesting :—

Theatre Royal in Drury Lane, this present Wednesday, being the 12th of November, will be presented a Comedy, call'd

THE INCONSTANT!

Capt. Duretete, Mr. Woodward ; Young Mirabel, Mr. Palmer ; Old Mirabel, Mr. Yates; Dugard, Mr. Blakes; Petit, Mr. Usher; Oriana, Mrs. Davies ; Lamorce, Mrs. Bennet ; Bizarre, Mrs. Clive.

To which will be added a New Grand Entertainment of
Dancing, call'd

THE CHINESE FESTIVAL!

Compos'd by Mr. Noverre.

The Characters by Mons. Delaistre, Sig. Baletti, Mr. Lauchery,
Mr. Noverre (jun.), Mr. Donnison, Mons. St. Leger, Mr. Shaw-
ford, Mr. Mathews, Mons. Pochee, Mons. L'Clert, Mr. Harrison,
Mr. Granier. Mr. Hust, Mons. Sarney, Mr. Walker, Mrs. Vernon,
Miss Noverre, Mr. Morris, Mr. Rooker,, Mr. Sturt, Mr. Atkins,
Mr. Ackman, Mr. Walker, Sig. Pietro, Mrs. Addison, Mrs. No-
verre, Mrs. Gibbons, Mad. Charon, Mad. Rousselet, Mrs. Preston,
Mad. Rouend, Mrs. Philips, Mrs. Lawson, The Little Pietro,
Miss Young, Master Simson, Master Pope, Master Blagden,
Master Hust, Master Spilsbury, Miss Bride, Miss Poplin, Miss
Simson, Miss Heath, Mr. Scrase, Mr. Lewis, Mr. Jefferson, Mr.
Burton, Mr. Marr, Mr. Vaughan, Mr. Chamness, Mr. Bullbrick,
Mr. Clough, Mr. Allen, Mr. Gray, Mrs. Bradshaw, Mrs. Hippis-
ley, Mrs. Mathews, Mrs. Simson, and Miss Mills.—With New
Music, Scenes, Machines, Habits, and other Decorations.

Boxes, 5s.; Pit, 3s.; First Gallery, 2s.; Upper Gallery, 1s.

Places for the Boxes to be had of Mr. Varney, at the Stage-
door of the Theatre.

₊ No persons can possibly be admitted behind the Scenes, or
into the Orchestra. Nothing under the Full Prices will be
taken during the whole performance.

Between her and one of the leading male performers
there also reigned a sort of hostility. This was that
excellent actor Woodward. His delightfully expressive
portrait looks down on us from the wall of the Garrick
Club. The fine face breathes the whole spirit of the
character, *The Copper Captain*; it is full of life and expression ; the reckless Bobadil-like carelessness and vigour,
the flourish with which the hat is set on, the air of flash
and the strut, are all admirable. But what strikes us

most is the sense of power, resource, fire, and entertainment
in his bold eye, and *bravura* of expression. Such a picture
is the best memorial, and indeed revives the play and
character for the spectator. There are but a few of such
histrionic presentments, among which might be counted
the fine full-length portrait of Lewis as *The Marquis*—a
picture breathing the whole spirit of gallant comedy : the
better known one of Garrick as *Abel Drugger*, matchless
for its expression of low wonder and cunning ; and above all
the scene from "The Clandestine Marriage," also in the
Garrick Club, with its wonderfully painted figure of *Lord
Ogleby*. There might perhaps be added that of Kemble as
Hamlet, by Sir Thomas Lawrence. The successful painter
in this line is nearly always a playgoer, not contenting
himself with conventional sittings, but fixing and carrying
away his impressions from the stage itself. Such were
Zoffany, De Wilde, Sir Martin Shee, and Clint.

Between Woodward and the actress there was a sort of
jealousy or lack of sympathy—which extended even to the
business of the scene. Neither seemed willing to co-operate
with the other, or the touchy actress fancied that he was
always struggling for "his own hand." The audience
were quite in the secret of this hostility, and were often
highly entertained by scenes between the pair.—Once in
January, 1756—during the performance of the "Taming
of the Shrew" then called "Catherine and Petruchio"—a
strange scene took place. As Woodward made his exit,
he actually threw down Mrs. Clive with such violence,
Wilkinson tells us "as to convince the audience that
Petruchio was not so lordly as he assumed to be." The
actress was so enraged at this rough treatment, that "her
talons, tongue, and passions were very expressive to the

I

eyes of all beholders, and it was with the utmost difficulty that she suppressed her indignation." Wilkinson seems to have witnessed the scene. Davies on another occasion, noted, that she seemed quite intimidated by his violence, as if by a tyrannical husband in real life. Once he stuck a fork into her finger! But the incidents are of so obstreperous a kind, that this must have been an accident. With such performers, the whole must have been a most entertaining spectacle. We could wish to see it revived by Irving and Miss Terry, not in this maimed farcical shape, but in the poetical form of the original, where *Sly's* vision offers one of the most dramatic contrasts conceivable.

Another passage occurred between the pair in the following year (1755), during the performance of "The Double Dealer," and which, Davies tell us, "caused such repeated laughter in the theatre as I scarcely ever heard"— no great test of anything very humorous; as the moving of audiences to laughter are often regulated by Swift's receipt, viz.: — the pulling away a chair when a person is about to sit down. Mrs. Clive, who performed *Lady Froth*, had by mistake, or in a hurry, laid on more rouge than usual; and *Brush, the valet*, played by Woodward, instead of saying "Your coachman, having a red face," said " *Your ladyship has a red face.*" This was no sooner uttered, than peals of laughter were redoubled all over the theatre. Woodward affected to look abashed and confounded: Clive bore the incident heroically. When they were in the green-room, the players expected a scene of altercation; but the inimitable actress disappointed them. "Come, Mr. Woodward," she gravely said, "let us rehearse the next scene, lest more blunders should fall out." In this *Lady Froth*, "Tom Davies," who was enthusiastic on her merits, protests she was superior to all actresses. " Happy the author who could write a part equal to her abilities ! She not only in general exceeded the writer's expectation, but all that the most enlightened could conceive."

In 1761, the town was entertained by a quarrel between Shuter, the "low" comedian, and the fiery actress, who thought she had been injured by him. She was always touchy about anything that related to her "benefit." On this occasion she had chosen a translated French piece,— "The Island of Slaves,"—and some one writing from the St. George's Coffee House, had addressed a malignant letter to the papers on this score. " He exhorts the public," she writes, " not to go to my benefit, because I was to have a French farce, wrote by a poor, wretched author. There is a malicious and wicked insinuation in his letter; and then with great malice and art, he jumbles together some popular words—such as French farce, English liberty, &c." This production, she chose to assume was the work of Shuter, and she attacked him with much fury. " I hope I may be indulged, though a woman, to say I have always despised the French Politics, but I never yet heard wo were at war with their wit : it should not be imputed to her, as a crime, to have a translation produced, when one part in three of all the comedies now acting are taken from the French, besides those of modern authors that have sneaked into the theatres without confessing from where they came." Unluckily she went on to ridicule Mr. Shuter's mode of composition. " It does not seem by the style of his letter, that he is very intimately acquainted with his own language, but it is evident he knows nothing

of French." It was Mrs. Clive's fate always to furnish
entertainment to the town, and to her reader also. Shuter
had a retort ready which caused much amusement. His
benefit he said had been most successful, "as usual, thanks
to the indulgence of the public; Mrs. Clive's I suppose
short of her expectations." Then, with malice, he printed
her letter, as a reply to her attack :—

"SIR.—I Much Desire you would Do Me the Favour to
let me know if you was the author of a letter in *The Dayle
Gazeteer* relating to his New Piece I had for my beuefet;
as it was intended to hurt my Benefet, and serve yours
everybody will naturely conclude you was the author if
you are not ashamed of being so I suppose you will own it:
if you really was not concerned in wrightin it I shall be
very glad : for I should be extreamly shock'd that an actor
should be guilty of so base an action ; I dont often take
the liberty of wrighting to the Publick but am Now under
a Nessity of Doing it—therefore Desier your answer.

"Henrietta street."

Shuter, to clear himself, actually swore an affadavit
before a magistrate that he was innocent.

But it was with her good-natured manager that this sort
of *fracas* most frequently occurred. The course of these
many wrangles offers a spectacle of high comedy, and
suggests the pleasant animosities of Benedick and Beatrix.
This hostility was maintained all through their twenty
years' relation. The superficial might suppose that a
deeply envenomed hatred was raging, and the actress
delighted in nothing so much as "plaguing" her manager
on every occasion. But it will be seen that in all this
bickering there was a real regard founded on a genuine

estoem, as indeed was to be expected between two such
sterling characters. As, indeed, it came out later, this was
but the "*amantium iræ!*" She was all the time, chafing
under what she thought was lack of recognition of her
powers, and had real admiration for her manager's talent.
She also resented his eagerness to put himself forward and
secure all the praise. "It was the wish of her life," says
the worthy Davies, "to act characters of importance with
him whenever *she could thrust herself* into a play with
him." How happily this expresses her character—"she
exerted her utmost skill to excel him—she was true game
to the last." On the other hand, in a droll contradictory
spirit, when she saw he was only striving for his own word,
she did her best to frustrate his efforts—fixing her eyes
on the audience and allowing them to wander to her friends
in the boxes, at his most critical passages—this she knew
would fret him and put him out. On other occasions when
she was in better humour she entertained herself with
comic "asides" to her companion; who, though rigid on all
matters connected with stage discipline, could not control
his muscles and had after to retire, being driven off the
stage. All this was of course improper, and a foolish
frowardness—but, as has been said, the secret was re-
vealed later.

CHAPTER V.

" Lady Riot."—Specimens of Bow China.—Dispute with Garrick.—Foote as " Othello," and Clive as "Portia."—"Bayes in Petticoats."—The Rosciad.—Lady Bab.—The Clandestine Marriage.

ONE of Clive's important characters, and always associated with her name, in which she took her farewell of the stage, was *Lady Riot*, the "fine lady" in "Lethe." This was an old farce of his own which he refitted entirely, introducing new characters,—an old nobleman, *Lord Chalkstone*, afflicted with gout,* a "fine gentleman" for Woodward, and this "fine lady" for Clive.—Evidence of the popularity of these two characters—Garrick was a failure—is found in the exquisite little figures of Bow china which were issued at the time, and have now become the rarest specimen of that manufacture. They are modelled with a charming grace and spirit. "Kitty" is shown in a monstrous petticoat, laces, and furbelows; while Woodward struts gaily, his enormous hat "cocked"—the very quintessence of a Town Beau. The pair of figures display much dramatic action, and are full of interest; and good specimens sell for nearly £30 a piece.

---

* Human infirmities should never be brought on the stage; indeed Elia has laid down that even the grosser failings of character, such as misers, &c., are to be excluded. When Dickens' "Christmas Carol" was in rehearsal, a realistic stage manager was for ordering a set of "irons" for *Tiny Tim*; but the amiable author took him aside,—"No," he said, "there may be parents in the audience to whom it would be painful."

The bringing out of this piece was attended by an unpleasant dispute with the manager. He had good-naturedly chosen it for her benefit, but the first deep offence was the mode of announcement in the bills. For here was to be seen only,

"The New Character of *Lord Chalkstone*, by MR. GARRICK!"

Her part was of course named, but not in the proper "displayed" style. "Madame Clive at noon came to the theatre," says Tate Wilkinson, "and furiously rang the alarm bell : for her name being omitted was an offence so serious, that nothing but 'blood!' was the word. Could she have got near him, and he had been severe in his replies, I daresay she would have disarranged his wig and dress. Mrs. Clive was a mixture of combustibles : she was passionate, cross, vulgar, yet sensible ; a very generous woman, and, as a comic actress, of genuine worth,—indeed, *indeed, indeed,* she was a diamond of the first water !" The sequel is admirably characteristic. She had great successes, a capital "reception," and her mimicry of the Italian singers was encored. In a moment all her humour vanished. "She came off the stage much sweetened in temper and manners from going on." "Ay !" she said in triumph "*that artful devil would not hurt me* with the town, though he had struck my name out of his bill." She laughed and joked about her late ill humour as if she could have kissed all around her. Though that happiness was not granted, but willingly excused, and what added to her applause, was her inward joy, triumph, and satisfaction, in finding the little great man was afraid to meet her, which was of all consolations the greatest." This happily sketched scene, showing a good knowledge of character, is rarely an epitome of the relations of this actress and her manager.

The bill speaks for itself, and shows that she *had* her proper place :—

Not acted these Ten Years.

FOR THE BENEFIT OF MRS. CLIVE.

At the Theatre Royal in Drury Lane, on Saturday next, being the 27th of March, 1756, will be revived a Comedy called

THE LADY'S LAST STAKE;

OR, THE WIFE'S RESENTMENT.

(Written by Colley Cibber, Esq.)

Lord George Brilliant, Mr. Woodward ; Lord Wronglove, Mr. Palmer; Sir Friendly Moral, Mr. Berry ; Lady Gentle, Mrs. Pritchard ; Mrs. Conquest, Mrs. Davies ; Miss Notable, Miss Macklin ; Hartshorn, Miss Minors ; and Lady Wronglove, by Mrs. CLIVE.

(Being the First Time of their Appearance in those Characters.)

To which will be added, a Dramatic Satire, called

LETHE !

In which will be introduced a New Modern Character, to be performed by Mr. GARRICK.

The Fine Lady ... ... Mrs. CLIVE.

In which will be introduced a New Mimic Italian Song.

Part of the Pit will be laid into the Boxes.

Another of her amusing creations, which gave scope for her unbounded humour, was in Foote's "Author," one of those unwarrantable personalities sketched from living persons, in which he revelled. In 1756, he was engaged in Drury Lane, and played often with Clive. One of these performances was his extraordinary attempt at *Othello*— with Clive in *Portia*—a combination of two mimics, which must have verged on burlesque. Cadwallader, was drawn from a Mr. Apreece, or Aprice—who had a trick of sucking his wrist as he spoke. Mrs. Clive was the wife, *Becky.* What the inimitable lady would have made of her character, aided by the humours of her acting, will be seen from his description of his spouse :—

"O Lord, Mr. Caper, this is Becky, my dear Becky! Child, this is a great poet,—ah, but she does not know what that is—a little foolish or so, but of a very good family. Here, Becky, child, wont you ask Mr. Caper to come and see you ?—Isn't she a fine girl ? Do come and look at her a little, do. He says you are as fine a woman as ever he ———. Then go talk any nonsense to her—no matter what—she's a great fool and wont know the difference."

The ridiculed gentleman, however, obtained an injunction from the Lord Chamberlain forbidding the piece, to the confusion and annoyance of the whole green-room. Foote, the frustrated mimic, was overwhelmed with despair and misery because he was not allowed to make others miserable; while Clive with piercing eyes and voice inveighed against her disappointment. A more serious lack of taste and decorum was shown in her attempt at *Portia* in the "Merchant of Venice,"—a character which she "discharged" not as originally *au serieux*, but in quite a burlesque spirit. In the Trial Scene she presented a *comic Portia*, and lighted the character by mimicking in it the manner of some leading counsel, such as Counsellor Dunning, whose peculiarities she "took off." The conjoined efforts of the pair must have made the play a rather ludicrous spectacle.

Unluckily she was too much addicted to such attempts,— another of which was her essaying *Bayes* in "The Rehearsal," which was a complete failure as a "breeches part." Like most born comedians, she had a hankering

K

after serious or even tragic characters.   These she fancied
she could discharge with ability and success.   It was thus
that for one of her benefits " the comic Clive put on the
Royal Robes of *Zara:* she found them too heavy, and
very wisely never attempted it again." *

It is to be suspected that the actress had always a fancy
for writing, from the letters and addresses she was fond of
addressing to the public ; and it must be said that her style
and matter is often excellent ; as in her letter to Garrick
on his retirement, which for feeling and description is of
the first class.   In 1753 she ventured to write and perform
a little two-act piece, which has at least smartness and
spirit ; it was called

THE REHEARSAL : OR, BAYS IN PETTICOATS ;
A Comedy in Two Acts, as it is performed at the Theatre
Royal in Drury Lane.   Written by Mrs. Clive ; the Music composed by Dr. Boyce.   1753.   Price One Shilling.   Published by
the Dodsleys.

It was ushered by a simple, straight-forward address, in
which the author, as usual, shows her honest pride in the
favour she enjoyed :

"This little Piece is as written above three Years since,
and acted for my Benefit.—The last Scene was an Addition
the year after : whatever Faults are in it, I hope will be

* It would be tedious to give a list of her characters which will
be found in the laborious collections of the Rev. Mr. Genest.   They
amount to almost two hundred !   How invaluable such variety of
characters must have been, may be well conceived.   We may
contrast with it the present unhappy system, whereby the young
actor is sent out into the country charged with a single character,
which he plays from town to town often for several years
together.

pardoned, when I inform the Public I had at first no Designe of printing it: and do it now at the Request of my Friends, who (as it met with so much indulgence from the audience) thought it might give some pleasure in the reading. The songs were written by a gentleman. I take this Opportunity to assure the Public, I am, with great Gratitude and Respect,

Their most Oblig'd,

Humble Servant,

C. CLIVE."

The performers were Woodward, Shuter, Cross, the prompter,—who appeared in his own character—Beard, and Miss Hoppisley. It seems to have been played about the year 1750. *Mrs. Hazard,* played by Clive, is bringing out a farce, and consults some fashionable visitors; as she is about to rehearse it, some importunate visitors come in and disturb the proceedings. But the trifle depends entirely on the smart dialogue, chiefly referring to her own personal relations with the audience, with hits at particular follies:

"But don't your heart ache," asks Willing, "when you think of the first night, hey?"

"Not in the least," she replies, "the town never hiss anything that is introduced to them by a person of consequence and breeding, because they are sure they'll have nothing low."

"Aye," he replies, "but they may'nt be so sure they'll have nothing foolish."

"Ha! why perhaps they may'nt find out one so soon as t'other, ha, ha, ha! well, let me die if that is not a very good thing! But it is well that the town don't hear me, not that I mean quite what I say, neither, for to do them justice, they're generally in the right in their censure."

They talk of the music, and she gives a hit at the manager:

"O, if dear Garrick could but sing, what a Don Quixote he'd make."

"Don't you think Barry would be a better? he's so tall you know, and so finely made for it.—I could take it to Covent Garden."

"Lord, I wouldn't think of it, it stands in such a bad air."

"Aye, the actors can't play there more than three times a week. They have more need of a physician than a poet at that house."

She then explains she has given one of the characters to Mrs. Clive:—

"I wish she don't spoil it, for she's so conceited and insolent that she won't let me teach it to her. You must know then, when I told her I had a part for her in a performance of mine in the prettiest manner I was able (for one must be civil to these sort of people, when one wants them,) says she, 'indeed madam, I must see the whole piece, for I shall take no part in a new thing without choosing that which I think I can act best. I have been a great sufferer already by the manager's not doing justice to my genius: but I hope I shall next year convince the town what fine judgment they have: for I intend to play a capital tragedy part for my own benefit.'"

A girl "Miss," comes in asking to be engaged to sing, and gives a specimen.—Mrs. Clive takes up her favourite subject of ridicule:—

"O fie, Miss! That will never do: you speak your words as plain as a parish girl: the audience will never endure you in this kind of singing; if you understand what they say. You must give your words the Italian accent, child."

She then mimics the singers. The scene now changes to the theatre, for the "Rehearsal," when Cross says :—

"The music has been here this half hour, and everybody but Mrs. Clive, and I dare say she'll not be long, for she's very punctual."

" Well Mr. Cross," she replies, " you have had a great deal of trouble with this thing : pray when is your benefit—you have a benefit I suppose? set me down all your side boxes and every first row in the front."

Cross then announces that :—

"Madam, Mrs. Clive, has sent word that she can't possibly wait on you this morning, as she is oblig'd to go to some ladies about her benefit ; but you may depend upon her being very perfect."

" Mr. Cross, what did you say? Mrs. Clive sent me word she can't come, and is gone to some ladies about her benefit! Sir, she shall have *no* benefit. Very fine indeed. To have the assurance to prefer her benefit to my 'Rehearsal.' Mr. Cross, you need not give yourself the trouble to set down any place for me at your benefit, for I'll never come into the playhouse any more."

A rehearsal of the music follows, when *Miss Giggle* breaks in, with a number of friends. They interrupt in the most annoying way, and finally the whole performance is given up. Thus the trifle ends.

It was in 1761, that Churchill threw the whole theatrical community into a state of alarm and indignation by his publication of the famous "Rosciad," in which the merits and defects of each player were sketched with a terrible vigour and truth. The small performers suffered the most : such as Tom Davies, who was told that he delivered his lines much as "a cur mouths a bone." Some obscure people were extravagantly praised ; some favourites as outrageously abused. The performers were in terror, as the burly ex-parson was seen "near the spikes of the orchestra " making his observations. Mrs. Clive and her friend Miss Pope, were let off with judicious praises. Not long before she retired, a contemptible imitator of Churchill published a similar gallery, entitled "Thespis," in which was a scurrillous attack upon our actress. After a malignant allusion to

"Clive's weak head and execrable heart,"

He goes on to describe her :—

"Formed for those coarse and vulgar soenes of life,
Where low-bred rudeness always breathes in strife ;
When in some blessed union we find
The deadliest temper with the narrowest mind,
The boldest front that never knew a fear,
The flintiest eye that never shed a tear,—
Then not an actress certainly alive
Can e'en dispute pre-eminence with CLIVE ! "

There can be no question but the authors of the "Rosciad" and of "Thespis," would in our time have been brought to the Law Courts, and have had to answer in damages for such libellous attacks.

One of her happiest creations was that of *Lady Bab* in that diverting piece, "High Life Below Stairs," which may be still said to hold the stage. This is true comedy, which it is impossible to witness without genuine enjoyment. It is founded on the folly and affectation not merely of one class, but on the general weakness of all, viz.: the aping the manners and ways of our betters. *My Lord Duke, Sir Harry*—how pleasant too the familiarity of *Bob, the Bishop*, an unseen member of the fraternity!—are all delightful. But the art of personating these characters is lost. The whole depends on the perfect genuineness of the assumption, with a sort of state and pretension. Ordinarily we are presented with servants of the existing type : there is no attempt to pourtray the stately, conceited, pampered menial, who wears his master's vices at second hand.

This merry piece has been generally ascribed to a master of Merchant Taylors School, the Rev. Mr. Townly : but it has also been considered Garrick's. The London footmen were an important body, and were often sent by their employers to keep places for them at the theatres; and Garrick would naturally shrink from having his name attached to such a piece of ridicule. It may be conceived that Mrs. Clive was at her best in this presentment of the "fine lady's maid." That this was a dangerous piece to bring forward was shown by its reception at Edinburgh, where all the menials of the town assembled in the gallery and brought about a regular riot.

Yet, another of her brilliant characters was that of *Mrs. Heidleberg*, the vulgar old maid, in "The Clandestine Marriage," a delightful comedy, but requiring to be performed by well-graced and well-trained comedians—nay, the very atmosphere of the theatre should be one of calm

high-class comedy, such as is found in the Theatre Français,
even before the curtain has risen. There should also be
the practice of years—when the details of the piece are
enriched by successive performances, and the players grow
with their characters. The composition of "The Clandestine Marriage" might be a study for our dramatists, for it
was literally written in the theatre. The characters as the
piece was constructed, actually bore only the names of the
actors—the manager contributed as much as the author.
How excellent the whole is may be seen from the fact that
the *French Valet* is one of the most important characters.
No servant should be introduced merely for the mechanical
functions of service—but for his share in the plot, or for
the development of other characters. In our own time it
is the fashion to open the play by the unmeaning device
of a conversation between two servants, who converse in
a supposed dialect of the servant's hall.

The bill of the performance is interesting as showing the
business-like character of the play bills :—

.THE FIFTEENTH NIGHT.

By His Majesty's Company, at the Theatre Royal in Drury
Lane, This present Thursday, the 10th April, will be presented
a New Comedy, call'd

THE CLANDESTINE MARRIAGE !

THE PRINCIPAL CHARACTERS BY

Mr. Holland, Mr. Powell, Mr. Yates, Mr. King, Mr. Palmer,
Mr. Love, Mr. Lee, Mr. Baddeley, Mr. Aickin, Mr. Watkins,
Miss Pope, Mrs. Palmer, Mrs. Abington, Miss Plym,
and Mrs. CLIVE.

Boxes, 5s.   Pit, 3s.   First Gallery, 2s.   Upper Gallery, 1s.

Places for the Boxes to be had of Mr. Johnston, at the Stage
Door.

₀ No Money to be received at the Stage Door nor any Money
returned after the Curtain is drawn up.

Vivant Rex et Rejina.

To-morrow, " KING JOHN," With the " CAPRICIOUS LOVERS."
For the Benefit of Mr. HAVARD.

CHAPTER VI.

Continued Wranglings with Garrick.—Correspondence.— Ill Spelling. — "Quaviling."—Fined for Absence.— "Acting a Gridiron."—Dr. Johnson.—Retirement from the Stage.

UNLUCKILY with advancing years the temper of our actress seemed to grow soured, and her sense of grievance, real or imaginary, more keen. She seemed to look out for opportunities of quarrel, and made herself as troublesome as she could. This unlucky spirit seems presently to have actually driven her to the resolution of retiring from the stage, when she was scarcely fifty-seven years old. A single specimen of the style in which she would comport herself in a wrangle of this sort, will be found highly entertaining, as exhibiting her frowardness and the placidity and tact of Mr. Garrick; indeed it proves what admirable gifts of "management," in the strictest sense, he possessed. The quarrel arose on the subject of the day of a benefit, on which the players were always touchy. The letters speak for themselves, and I have retained the bad spelling for which "Kitty" was famous, as an additional contribution to the reader's amusement.*

---

* Some of these curious letters will be found in the Forster MSS. at South Kensington; some were published by Mr. J. Fitzgerald Molloy, in a Sketch of Mrs. Clive's career.

MRS. CLIVE TO THE MANAGERS.

"Feb. 13, 2 o'clock.

"GENTLEMEN.—I am advised (I may say it is insisted in by my best friends) not to be a dupe to your ill treatment of me, by giving up above half of my income at a time when I know I can have no alternetive. I know tis in in vain to Expostulate with people in power : whether I am injured or not will appear to all who are *imparsial* : as to your. sneering me about my consequence, you may take what steps you please with your power, but you can't mortifie me. Tis *nessesary* to explain one thing which may be convenient to be forgot by you, that when Mr. Lacy agreed with me in the summer he gave me his word that everything relating to my engagement this season shou'd stand as it did in my last article, where my Benefit is *perticularised* to be on or before the 17 of March ; of the truth of this I will take my oath. As to Mr. Woodward insisting upon haveing my day, he may insist on haveing part of my Sallery—I have nothing to doe with him, and have behaved allways to the managers of the Play-house I belong'd to, in an honest and open manner, never haveing had *scheems* or Desings to undermine or disapiont them in there business. Therefore whatever mine may be, you shan't have it to say I took the advantage of Mrs. Pritchard's illness to distress your Plays. As to my Benefit you shall do as you please, as I have no written agreement.

I am, gent.,

Your Servt.,

C. CLIVE."

MR. GARRICK'S ANSWER.

"DEAR MADAM. — You always choose to have some
quarrel at your benefit, and without reason; but I do not.
I am surprised that you have not thanked the managers
for this kindness, instead of writing so peevish a letter.
Your benefit is now settled upon the best day of the week,
and six days sooner than you were last year. This was
meant kindly for you, and every lady must see it in that
light. I shall be sorry that you will not accept of that
day (as you are pleased to say), because I wish you well,
and it will be of great service to you: therefore if you will
not advertise and fix your play, your folly be upon your
own head. I cannot do more than I have done for you,
and your friends must blame you.

I am, dear madam,

Your humble servant,

Friday night, 14 Feb., 1768.   D. G."

MRS. CLIVE TO THE MANAGERS.

"SIR.—I am much surprised to hear that you have fixed
the 17 of March for my Benefit, and that Mrs. Dancer is
to have the Monday before (which as Mr. Hopkins tells me
was designed for Mr. Barry.) I hope I shall not be guilty
of vanity in saying that upon Drury Lane Theatre, *nither*
Mr. Barry nor Mrs. Dancer have a right to their Benefits
before me. I have done you great service this season, and
at every call, when they either cou'd not, or wou'd not
play, have been the stop gap in playing *principle* parts—
and even when I have been extremely ill; I do not suppose
that expostulation will have any effect to alter what you
and the Lady have been pleased to settle. Therefore all I

mean by giving you this trouble, is to assure you I will not accept of that day, nor will I advertise for it. If I am wrong in this determination, I may *loose* my friends, and they will naturally think you have acted onorably. (?)

Your humble Servt.,

Friday, Feb. 18, 1768.   C. CLIVE."

MRS. CLIVE TO MR. GARRICK.

"Feb. 19, 1768.

"SIR.—I am sorry to give you this trouble, but I really cannot comprehend what you mean by saying you exspected I should thanke the managers for their tenderness to me. I have allways been greatfull to every one who has obliged me, and if you will be so good as to point out the obligations I have to you and Mr. Lacy, I shall have great pleasure in acknowledging them. You tell me you have done all you *can* for me, and you *can* do *more*. I don't know how to understand that. Any one who sees your letter wou'd suppose I was kept at your Theatre out of Charitey. If you still look over the number of times I have play'd this season—you must think I have desarvd the mouney you give me. You say you give me the best day in the week. I am sorry to say I cannot be of your opinion. St. Patrick's Day is the very worst to me that can be. Mrs. Yates' might be the strongest Benefit, as her interest and mine clash in the Box's. As to my *quaviling* you are under a very great misstake. There is nothing I dread so much, I have not spirits for that, tho' have for acting. You say that you have fixt the day, and have drawn a line under it that I may be sure I can have no other : therefore I must take it—But I must think it (and so will every impartial person) very hard that Mrs. Dancer should have her Benefit before Mrs. Clive. You may depend upon having no further trouble with me. Indeed, I flattered myself that as the greatest part was past of the season, and I had done everything you asked of me, in playing a very insignificant part on purpose to please you, *I say*, I was in hope's it would have ended as it had gone so far, without any unkindness. But I shall say no more than that

I am, Sir,

Your most humble servt.,

C. CLIVE."

MR. GARRICK TO MRS. CLIVE.

"Saturday.

" DEAR CLIVE.—How can you be so ridiculous, and still so cross, to mistake every word of my letter, that I could have so low a thought as you suggest about *charity*, and which I am ashamed to read in yours. *The insignificant part* which you said you acted to oblige me, is very insignificant indeed as well as the piece it is in, so you have endeavoured to be rude to me without effect—you speak of these things, just as you are *in* or *out* of humour; so it shall stand for nothing. However, I have such a regard for you, that I promise you for the future, you shall be no more troubled with any nonsense of mine, and I am rejoiced that you have cancelled the obligation you say you conferred upon me by accepting the part, by ungenteely telling me of it. You will find in your present humour objections to any day, but we really meant you *kindly* in giving you your own day, that you might avoid opera nights, and have nobody to come immediately before or after you. This I did not do out of *charity*, but out of that respect which I ever pay to genius, and it is not my fault if Mrs. Clive will not be as rational off the stage, as she is meritorious on it.

I am, my dear madam,

Your most sincere well wisher and servant,

D. GARRICK."

P.S.—I drew a line under the day in speaking of it as I wrote in your own words, and not with any other intention. It is impossible to mistake it.

All which is truly entertaining, and "quaviling" is an original form ; but the grievance rankled. It is droll to note how in her letters the sense of injury worked itself off, and when she had expended her vexation in some smart biting phrases, she was only too ready to lower her colours.

Her perverseness, no doubt, gave Mr. Garrick a vast deal of anxiety and annoyance—so much so that, it was well known, he came to dread an altercation with her as much as with an actor. Any yielding or complaisance, he had to obtain by humouring her, or by compensation, sooner than have the usual wrangle. As when she grew old and was unsuited to the character of *Miss Price* in "Love and Love"—a girl of sixteen—he could only "get it from " her by giving her the more important character of *Mrs. Frail*—to which, however, she was equally un-suited. Nor had she much sense of restraint or decorum in expressing her feelings. As when on the first night of the ranting piece, "Barbarossa," he entered the green-room arrayed in all his Eastern finery, expecting the flatteries of the company, she coarsely said, "Make room for the Royal Lamplighter," a rude speech which quite overset him, as well it might.

Once, "The Devil to Pay," was announced unexpectedly, when the actress was dining in the country with some persons of quality. She arrived too late, and was fined. She resented, not the fine, but the implied failure in her duty. Her defence is irresistible, and in her best style.

"I have great regret," she wrote, "in being obliged to say anything that looks like contention. I wish to be quiet myself, and I am sure I never laid any scheme in my life to make any one uneasy or unhappy. In regard to the affair of 'The Devil to Pay,' I sent in complaints to the managers by the prompter, to beg that it might not be done till the weather was cool, as the quickness of the shift puts me in a flurry, which gives me a violent swimming of the head. I beg you would do me the favour to let me know if it was by your order my money was stopped last Saturday. You was so good indeed last week to bid me take *care* or I should be catched—I thought you was laughing, I did not know it was a determined thing. It was never before expected of a performer to be in waiting when their names are not in the *papers* or *bills;* the public are witness for me whether I have ever neglected my business. You may (if you please to recollect) remember I have never disappointed you four times since you have been a manager; I always have had good health, and have ever been above subterfuge. I hope this stopping of money is not a French fashion; I believe you will not find any part of the English laws that will support this sort of treatment of an actress, who has a right, from her character and service on the stage, to expect some kind of respect. I have never received any favours from you or Mr. Lacy, nor shall ever ask any of you, therefore hope you will be so good to excuse me for endeavouring to defend myself from what I think an injury; it has been too often repeated to submit to it any longer. You stopped four days' salary when I went to Dublin, though you gave me leave to go before the house shut up, and said you would do without me. If I had known your intention, I would not have lost any of my salary, as my agreement with Mr. Barry did not begin till our house had shut up. I had my money last stopped at the beginning of the season for not coming to rehearse two parts that I could repeat in my sleep, and which must have cost two guineas, besides the pleasure of coming to town.

"When I was sent to, I recollected I had given my servant leave to go out, as I did not want her, who had the key of all my things: neither had I the necessary things ready if she had been at home. I had a friend's equipage come for me for Greenwich, to dine with them, and take my leave, as they are going to Bath. I was very unhappy after I was there, and the gentleman was so obliging as to send one of his grooms at half-an-hour after four, to let you know I would come if you could not do without me. I had a carriage ready with the horses put to, when he came back – it wanted then some minutes to six. It is very happy for me that they happen to be people of consequence, who know the truth of what I say, and who will be very much surprised to hear how I have been treated.

"I am sure I have always done everything in my power to serve and oblige you : the first I have most undoubtedly succeeded in : the latter I have always been unfortunately unsuccessful in, though I have taken infinite pains. I have never envied you your equipage, nor grandeur, the fine fortune you have already and must be still increasing. I have had but a very small share of the public money. You

gave Mrs. Cibber £600 for playing sixty nights, and £300
to me for playing 180, out of which I can make it appear
it cost me £100 in necessaries for the stage ; sure you need
not want to take anything from it."

We may be sure that the fine was remitted.

Mr. John Taylor, long one of the editors of the *Sun*,
and who knew most of the actors, suggests, that as she
was eminent before Garrick's appearance, his love of
excellence threw her and others in the shade, and she therefore took every opportunity of venting her spleen.   This
was only the popular view.   "One night" he tells us "as
he was performing *King Lear*, she stood behind the scenes
to observe him, and in spite of the roughness of her nature,
was so deeply affected, that she sobbed one minute and
abused him the next, and at length overcome by his
pathetic touches, she hurried from the place with the
following extraordinary tribute to the universality of his
powers, 'D—n him, I believe he could act a gridiron.'"

This contention is often found when there is real regard.

The excellent Dr. Johnson, who knew most of the
guild, and supported Mrs. Abington's benefit, highly
esteemed our actress.   So sterling a nature had the true
instinct for appreciating what was sterling in others.   "He
used, at one time, to go occasionally to the green-room
of Drury Lane Theatre, where he was much regarded
by the players, and was very easy and facetious with
them."   This is Mr. Langton's account.   "He had a very
high opinion of Mrs. Clive's comic powers, and conversed
with her more than with any of them."   He said, "Clive
is a grand thing to sit by, she always understands what
you say."   "A good thing to sit by," was no light praise

from the Doctor, and she said of him "I love to sit by Dr. Johnson, he always entertains me." His judicial opinion upon her acting was equally favourable. "Mrs. Porter in her vehemence of rage, and Mrs. Clive in the sprightliness of humour, I have never seen equalled. What Clive did best, she did better than Garrick; but she could not do half so many things well; she was a better romp than any I ever saw in nature." This nice distinction shows how admirable a critic Johnson was. Here he was surely right; for the romp on the stage should be better than any in nature; as histrionic characters should not aim at mere imitation, but at the selection of the best points.*

Only a few months later we find her in the most gracious mood. And here again we see the sensitiveness of a regard which she believed was unrequited. On Nov. 27, 1768, she writes :—

"Dear Sir,—I am most extremely obliged to you for your very polite letter. How charming you can be when you are good; I believe there is only one person in the world who has never known the difference.† I shall certainly make use of the favour you offer me; it gives me a double pleasure—the entertainment my friends will receive

---

* When everyone was praising Garrick's *Archer*, in the disguise of a "footman," how admirably he did the servant, "you would take him for a real one,"—"No! no!" said the sage "it is not a good performance, he does not let the gentleman break out through the footman." This is real dramatic criticism, and instruction for the actor, of the highest order.   .

† The manager has endorsed this—
        "A love-letter—the first I ever had
        from that truly great comedian, Mrs. Clive."

from your performance, and the being convinced that you have a sort of sneaking kindness for your Pivy. I suppose I shall have you tapping me on the shoulder (as you do to *Violante*) when I bid you farewell, and desiring one tender look before we part, though perhaps you may recollect and toss the pancake into the cinders. You see I never forget your good things. Pray make my best compliments to Mrs. Garrick, and believe I shall always have sincere pleasure when I can assure you

I am, your obliged and humble servant,

C. CLIVE."

It must be confessed there is a peculiar entertainment in this production, a delicacy, and truth, surprising in one commonly believed to have been of a coarse temperament.

When she had finally made up her mind to depart from the theatre, she made a last display of frowardness. It seems likely that this was owing to a sense of pique and wounded pride, for she expected, no doubt, that great exertions would be made to detain her. Garrick, however, in most instances, was inclined to take his actors at their word, and was, perhaps, relieved at the idea of being released from their ceaseless jars and discussions. This soreness was shown in the ungraciousness in which the actress announced her departure. When it came to the point, however, he deputed his prompter, Hopkins, to ask if she were serious ; to him she disdained to give any satisfaction. Geo. Garrick, the stage manager, was next sent, but she told him bluntly that the manager himself must come, if he wished to learn her sentiments. Mr. Garrick arrived, and with many compliments on her services, hoped that for her own sake, she would remain. She scornfully

hinted that he meant his own interest. He then asked
" How much she was worth?" meaning what she valued
her services at. She answered briskly, " as much as himself." He, with a smile, assured her that he had not put
by so much as she fancied ; when she answered him that
" she knew when she had enough, but he never did."
After this display of rude temper, the complacent manager
again begged of her to change her mind, and stay with
them for a few years longer. But she bluntly refused : she
was tired of the trouble and annoyance of stage life. On
which he prepared to take his leave, assuring her that he
deeply regretted her loss ; when, with a last burst, she
said, " she hated hypocrisy," and that " she knew he would
light up candles for joy at her going, only for the money it
would cost him." Here again we see only the vexation of
a jealous spirit. The Drury Lane green-room was filled
with gossips of the Tate Wilkinson pattern, and particularly
with dissatisfied ladies, who were glad to repeat Mr. Garrick's
presumed speeches and opinions. Long after she solemnly
made confession that all this time he had no greater and
more genuine admirer.

As was to be expected, Garrick did all he could to gratify
the actress, in what he would have called " her last
moments." He offered to play for her in one of his best
characters. This favour she acknowledged affectionately,
though a little tartness breaks out in her allusion to her
husband.

MRS. CLIVE TO MR. GARRICK.

" London, April 14th; 1769.

" DEAR SIR.—I could not stay till the 24th to thank you
for your very kind letter. I am extremely glad to hear

you continuo to be so well. I have often enquired after you of your brother George : now do not say to yourself, ay, for your own sake; for when I heard you was in such great pain, I was most sincerely sorry. In the next place, to bo sure, I am *glad* you are well for the sake of my audience, who will have the pleasure to see their own Don Felix. What signifies fifty-two? they had rather see *the* Garrick and *the* Clive at a hundred and four, than any of the moderns;—the ancients, you know, have always been admired. I do assure you, I am at present in such health and such spirits, that when I recollect I am an old woman, I am astonished. My dear town are giving me such applause every time they see me, that I am in great fear for myself on my benefit night; I shall be overcome with kindness. Indeed, I have every day fresh instances of the public affection for me. Lord Clive has behaved in a noble manner; he sent me the most polite note, and fifty pounds · for his box. I am greatly obliged to Sir William Stanhope: if he should be at Bath when you receive this, I beg you would do me the favour to return my thanks to him ; I hope I shall have the pleasure of doing it at Twickenham. You are very much mistaken if you imagine I shall be sorry to hear Mr. Clive is well; I thank God I have no malice or hatred to any body : besides, it is so long ago since I thought he used mo ill, that I have quite forgot it. I am glad ho is well and happy.

"Pray make my best respects to Mrs Garrick, who I hope is so well as not to want the waters.

I am, dear Sir,

Your most sincere friend and humble servant,

C. CLIVE."

Clive was not one of the class who make their farewell bow only to return.—She had formed her resolution to retire, in the plenitude of her powers, and adhered to it. She was now but fifty-eight years old, and might have entertained the town for fully ten years more, with mutual advantage.   But she knew the truth of the line :

> " Inglorious lags the veteran on the stage."

—whether the stage be one of politics, or any other.

The night fixed was April 24, and the plays were " The Wonder "—which Garrick also chose for his own departing effort—with " Lethe "—and in which she gave her incomparable " Fine Lady."—The rush for places was enormous. As the bill has it ; " No tickets have been given out but to those ladies and gentlemen who have the places secured in the pit and boxes ; and to prevent any mistake or confusion, no box tickets will be admitted into the gallery. Mrs. Clive begs the favour of those whose places are in the pit to be there by half-an-hour after five, and to let their servants come to keep them a quarter before four.   Pit and boxes laid together."—That is, the pit was charged at box price.

Mr. Garrick played, and played his best we may be sure. In both pieces Mr. Walpole furnished an epilogue, a form of relation between audience and actor (better surely than the speech now in fashion) which has long passed away.

> With glory satiate, from the bustling stage,
> Still in his prime—and much about my age,
> *Imperial* Charles (if Robertson says true)
> Retiring, bade the jarring world adieu !
> Thus I, long honoured with your partial praise,
> (A debt my swelling heart with tears repays !

Scarce can I speak—forgive the grateful pause)
Resign the noblest triumph, your applause.
Content with humble means, yet proud to own,
I owe my pittance to your smiles alone ;
To private shades I bear the golden prize,
The meed of favour in a nation's eyes ;
A nation brave, and sensible, and free—
Poor Charles ! how little when compar'd to me !
His mad ambition had disturb'd the globe,
And sanguine which he quitted was the robe.
Too blest, could he have dar'd to tell mankind,
When power's full goblet he forbore to quaff,
That, conscious of benevolence of mind,
For thirty years he had but made them laugh.
Ill was that mind with sweet retirement pleased, ·
The very cloister that he sought he teazed ;
And sick, at once, both of himself and peace,
He died a martyr to unwelcome ease.
Here ends the parallel, my generous friends,
My exit no such tragic fate attends ;
I will not die—let no vain panic seize you—
If I repent, I'll come again and please you.

That last sight of the audience, nightly friends and
companions for many years—a part of life itself—must
be a painful moment.   Garrick declared that the thought
was agony, and a sort of theatrical *death*.   More acute still
must be the feelings in the dull monotonous evenings
that follow.   Mrs. Siddons, as the night drew on,
would repeat. with a sort of wistful distress, " Now
they are filling the theatre ! Now the curtain has risen."
She would recall the uproar that used to greet her.
It was like the chill on waking from a delightful
dream.   Now there was only an old lady seated by her
humdrum fireside.

CHAPTER VII.

Twickenham.—Little Strawberry Hill.—"Jemmy Raftor."
—Friendship with Walpole. —Miss Pope.

IT has been generally repeated that on her retirement
from the stage, Mr. Walpole invited her to take possession of a small house at Twickenham, where she resided for
the rest of her life. The fact is, this generous present was
made to her nearly twenty years before, and we find her
living at "little Strawberry Hill" so early as 1753 or 1754.
Walpole had a genuine and steady regard for her, founded
perhaps on the enjoyment of her society, for her ready wit
and stories entertained him. She was a constant guest at
his house, the companion of his walks, and often enjoyed
his hospitality at little suppers.

We now see the favourite actress retired, and living
altogether at pleasant Twickenham. After "the youth of
folly," came "an old age of cards," of agreeable society—
gossip it might be—and cordial friends. It is not generally
known that before taking up her abode at little Strawberry
Hill, she was established at a cottage of Mr. Walpole's,
known as "little Marble Hill," long since pulled down, its
place being taken by a pretentious mansion. This had
been her residence till little Strawberry Hill was got ready
for her.

The house which Mr. Walpole so handsomely presented
to his friend is still to be seen on the road-side, a little
beyond the old town of Twickenham, and facing the
meadows across which he so often walked to pay her a

visit. An old and rather decayed red brick structure, two
stories in height, with stabling and gardens attached, and
altogether of more pretension than would be imagined from
the description. We can identify it by the arched sham
Gothic windows, in the style of old Strawberry Hill. The
gate displays two great stone acorns, but the whole has
been rather disfigured by modern additions.—It is indeed
quite an historical residence. After her death, he persuaded the attractive Misses Berry—pets and *protegées* of
his—to take up their residence there. They remained for
many years and were an inexpressible source of comfort and
entertainment to their host. Twickenham, when Clive
first went to reside, had quite a number of remarkable
people living there :—Sir John Hawkins, Lady Tweeddale,
George Steevens, and others. She had, therefore, plenty of
friends and acquaintances to make her retirement at this
old fashioned place pleasant.*

Here we find a member of the family—her brother,
James Raftor, "Jemmy," as he was called, to whom the
worthy Clive had clung all her life. She had again and
again given him benefits, played for him, and tried to get
him on—but fruitlessly. He was, as Lord Nuneham described him, "a wretched actor, hideous in person and pace,

---

* The writer, when a boy, lived close to Twickenham, and re-
calls the choice and pleasant society—mostly of a literary cast—
then found there. In that quaint row of antique houses of Queen
Anne's time, now in decay, lived a sister of Horace Smith, who had
often heard Miss Pope talk of her friend Clive and her glories. I
was then in a sort of fashion : the "Jerry Builder" had not come
that way, and it was but little altered from the time of Clive. At
every turn there were old fashioned houses, old inns, and footpaths
across the meadows ; while in all the "great houses," distinguished
tenants were residing.

N

and vulgarly awkward in his general appearance—but a
man of some information, of much observation and possessing an extraordinary fund of original humour. In his
talent of relating a story he was unrivalled." One of his
stories no doubt he told with humour, that of a town
lady,—who being asked why she did not live in the country,
said "she had just bought some *rural* object—a cuckoo
clock!" This entertaining fellow attracted Mr. Walpole, who conceived quite a friendship for him, and always
asked him with his more-gifted sister. "Raftor," he says
in 1770, "has left the stage: Mrs. Clive has very kindly
taken him to live entirely with her, and I hear he is
exceedingly happy at it."

At all *petits soupers* Mr. Raftor figured. No matter how
fine the company, there the brother and sister were to be
found. Even at the Coronation, when seats were so eagerly
sought, Walpole found him a place at his town house,
among the noble ladies. When Twickenham was scared
by highway robberies,—people being stopped on the roads,
and Mrs. Clive's house broken into—he declared that he
would make Raftor his Sancho Panza—"only he has more
humour." In 1753, he writes:—"I met Mrs. Clive two
nights ago, and told her I had been in the meadows, but
would walk no more there, for here was her world." "Well"
says she "and don't you like the World. I hear it was very
clever last Thursday." And again in 1754 : "My chief
employ is planting at Mrs Clive's, whither I remove all my
superabundancies. I have lately planted the green lane
that leads from her garden to the common." "Well" said
she "when it is done, what shall we call it?" "Why" said
I "what would you call it but Drury Lane?" This was
ready pleasantry. Later, when she was regularly installed,

for during her theatrical career she only came there after the
season, he gave the little *maison* the happy name of
Cliveden. When such guests as Mr. Conway, and Lady
Ailesbury, and Lady Townshend, were staying with
him, he would take them over to see the actress, and
sup with her. Lady Townshend, notorious for her strange
coarse speeches, being taken over Strawberry Hill, said
to the host, "that it would be a very pleasant place,
if Mrs. Clive's face did not rise upon it and make it so hot."
One evening in 1760, he met an odd adventure in one
of their walks, which is described in his best style.
"I was sitting with Mrs. Clive, her sister and brother, on
the bench near the road, at the end of her long walk. We
heard a violent scolding, and looking out saw a pretty
woman, standing by a high chaise, in which was a
young fellow and the coachman riding. The damsel
had lost her hat, her cloak, her temper, and her
senses; and was more drunk, and more angry, than you
can conceive. She stood cursing and swearing at the
young man in an outrageous style, and when she had
vented all the oaths she could think of, she at last
wished *perfidion* might seize him. You may imagine how
we laughed. The fair intoxicate turned round and cried,
'Who is it! What! Mrs. Clive! Kitty Clive! No, Kitty
Clive would never behave so.' I wish you could have seen
my neighbour's confusion. She certainly did not grow
paler than ordinary." Occasionally he could be merry at
the expense of his friend's full-blown face. She had been
left a legacy by a neighbour, Lord Radnor, only fifty
pounds, but was immensely elated. "You never saw
anything so droll" he writes "as Mrs. Clive's countenance,"
is the good natured remark of Walpole, on this event,

"between the heat of the summer, the pride in her legacy, and her efforts to appear concerned."

In the year 1760, she gave him an agreeable supper, "with Miss West, my niece Cholmondely, and Murphy, the writing actor, who is very good company, and two or three more. Mrs. Cholmondely is very lively, you know how entertaining the Clive is." Mrs. Cholmondely we may assume was Peg Woffington's rather boisterous sister.

She had at this time some faithful friends whose regard was the solace of her decline. There was her trusty brother, Mr. Walpole, and her "dear Pope." " Easy natural Miss Pope," cried Elia, as he dwelt on her part in "The School for Scandal," the original *Mrs. Candour*, a title to boast of. She was in fact Clive's pupil, who having a fancy for her from the first, took immense pains to school her in the true tradition. This admirable actress of the good old solid school was so intimately connected with her friend in every department, that she was considered a sort of reflection of Clive's character and talent. There was the same honest independence—the same sense of duty to their profession—the same clear and open good sense in both their lives. A true affection and sympathy bound them together to the last. There was no jealousy in Clive's nature, and she saw her friend take over her own characters with satisfaction, and was eager that she should make as good an impression as herself. " What principally matured her talents was to have found so excellent a model before her as Mrs. Clive," says a contemporary account " being in this actress's walk, she had the advantage of copying her inimitable manner and humour ; and though the ascent was great, emulation was still greater.

"Mrs. Clive *being on the retiring plan* almost on Miss Pope's commencement, gave her an opportunity to be let occasionally into some of the former's principal parts; such as *Phillis* in 'The Conscious Lovers,' *Beatrice* in 'Much Ado about Nothing,' &c.; each of which she was received in with particular compliment. But what called out the full extent of her powers, was the character of *Nell*, in Coffey's ballad farce of 'The Devil to Pay;' a circumstance the more remarkable, as it was in this very part, thirty years before, that Mrs. Clive gained the summit of her reputation. Though this at first looked against her, yet it turned out a point in her favour. Those who had seen Mrs. Clive in the character, or remembered her first appearance in it, were pleased with the thoughts of so able a successor."—Churchill was more enthusiastic on her merits than he was about Clive :—

> " With all the native vigour of sixteen,
> Among the merry troop conspicuous seen,
> See lively Pope advance in jig and trip
> Corinna, Cherry, Honeycomb, and Snip.
> Not without art, but yet to nature true,
> She charms the town with humour just yet new.
> Cheer'd by her promise we the less deplore
> *The fatal time when Clive shall be no more.*"

The lines "not without art," &c., should be the comedian's guide.

"I well remember" says Wilkinson, who was present, "on the second night of 'The Confederacy,' Mrs. Clive called Miss Pope into the green room, before her going on the stage as *Corinna*, and said to her, "My dear Pope,"—a sweet appellation indeed from Clive—"you played particularly well on Saturday, as a young actress, but take from me a piece of advice, which I would have every performer attend to.   You acted with great and deserved approbation, but to-night you must endeavour to act better, and expect to receive less applause.   The violent thunder of applause last Saturday, on your first appearance, was not all deserved, it was only benevolently bestowed to give you the pleasing information that they were well delighted, and had their warmest wishes that you would hereafter merit the kindness they bestowed you."   This plain spoken useful piece of advice was not thrown away, and would be found not unprofitable by all performers.

Once, on the eve of Garrick's retirement, the sensible Miss Pope was betrayed into a little foolishness, which was unlike her usual self.   All her companions were worrying the manager with their claims and complaints. After many years' service, when the formality of renewing her engagement, as a matter of course, was suggested, she wrote to ask for an increase of salary.   The managers replied with compliments on the value of her talents,—her place would be with difficulty supplied—and trusting she would continue with them as before.   She wrote back in irritation, that as to her merit it had been more than overpaid by the public, without even a paragraph to prejudice them.   She would put aside affection and think only, like the Swiss, of pay.   She received a rather cold reply to this taunt, with a reminder that they had lost Mrs. Barry from wishing to keep her, and declining to make any advance.   The actress indignantly left the theatre.   It was plain there was here some other grievance. But as the season drew on and she found herself without an engagement at the great theatre, she repented.

of her folly, and applied to her friend Clive, to bring about a reconciliation, who sent "Jimmy" Raftor to the manager. But he declined to receive her back. She applied to him herself in a very strong letter. She accused herself of a foolish vanity, but her heart was not bad. "As I know of no excuse to palliate my wrong conduct, I must rely upon your generosity still, to forgive and be my friend." But Garrick was inflexible.   As the Duke of Wellington put it later: "It was no mistake, and should be no mistake." "The expressions 'want of affection,' 'turning Swiss,'" he said "were as harsh as unexpected, and had given him great pain;" what rankled deeper, though he did not name it, was the allusion to newspaper puffs. Even, after his answer, he had waited two months, hoping she might see her mistake and return to her duty, and this in spite of her incivility to one who had always been her best friend.   Now her place was filled.   He was deeply grieved.   The actress submitted, and with a heavy heart went to Ireland.   But her case was in the hands of a faithful ally.   The irresistible Kitty took up the affair, as if it were her own, and was not to be denied.   Never was cause pleaded so effectively.   In a charming natural letter of compliment to him, on his impending retirement, which would have done credit to one of the professional letter writers, she appeals to him for the unfortunate Pope.

"Now let me say one word about my poor unfortunate friend, Miss Pope, I know how much she disobliged you, and if I had been in your place, I believe I should have acted just as you did.   But by this time I hope you have forgot your resentment and will look upon her late behaviour, as having been taken with a dreadful fit of vanity, which for the time took her senses from her,

and having been tutored by an affected heart, which helped
to turn her head ; but recollect her in the other light,
a faithful creature to you, on whom you could always
depend, certainly a good actress, amiable in her character,
both in being a very modest woman, and very good to
her family, and to my certain knowledge, has the
greatest regard for you.   Now my dear Mr. Garrick,
I hope it is not yet too late to reinstate her before
you quit your affairs here.   I beg it ! I entreat it ! I shall
look on it as the greatest favour you can confer on

Your ever obliged friend,

C. CLIVE."

This we find endorsed " My Pivy excellent ! "

Need it be said that Garrick did not reject the suit of
his faithful Pivy.   The glad news of her forgiveness and
restoration was despatched to the actress, who was even
bidden to name her own terms.   No wonder she wrote that
her heart was full, and that she could not express her
feelings.   She was his prodigal daughter, and was out of
her senses with happiness.   The whole credit was owing to
the worthy honest Clive.

Garrick's own retirement, as we have said, was now at
hand, and she took the opportunity to unfold to him, in
characteristic style—what, perhaps, he never suspected
before, viz.:—that through all their bickerings, it was not
dislike or disdain that was at work ; it was her pride that
would not bend to own his superiority and many good
qualities.   " D—n him, he can act a gridiron ! ". was but a
partial expression of her admiration.   We have smiled at
her rude turns and sad spelling, but here nature and
warmth of heart furnished her with an admirable style :—

MRS. CLIVE TO MR. GARRICK.

"Twickenham, June 23, 1776.

" Dear Sir.—Is it really true that you have put an end
to the glory of Drury Lane Theatre? *If it is so*, let me
congratulate my dear Mr. and Mrs. Garrick on their ap-
proaching happiness : *I know* what it will be ; you cannot
yet have an idea of it ; *but* if you should still be so wicked
not to be satisfied with that *unbounded*, uncommon degree
of fame you have received as an actor, and which no other
actor ever did receive—nor no other actor ever *can* receive ;
—I say, if you should still long to be dipping your fingers
in their theatrical pudding (now without plums), you will
be no Garrick for the Pivy.   In the height of public admiration for you, when you were never mentioned with any
other appellation but Mr. Garrick, the charming man, the
fine fellow, the delightful creature, both by men and ladies ;
when they were admiring everything you did and everything you scribbled, at this very time *The Pivy* was a
living witness that they did not know, nor could they
be sensible of half your perfections.   I have seen you with
your magical hammer in your hand, endeavouring to beat
your ideas into the heads of creatures who had none of
their own.   I have seen you with lamb-like patience,
endeavouring to make them comprehend you, and I have
seen you when that could not be done.   I have seen your
lamb turned into a lion : by this your great labour and
pains the public was entertained ; they thought they all
acted very fine—they did not see you pull the wires.

"There are people now on the stage to whom you gave
their consequence ; they think themselves very great,
now let them go on in their new parts without your leading

o

strings, and they will soon convince the world what this genius is. I have always said this to everybody, even when your horses and mine were in their highest prancing. While I was under your control I did not say half the fine things I thought of you, because it looked like flattering, and you know your Pivy was always proud, besides I thought you did not like me then, but now I am sure you do, which made me send this letter."

CHAPTER VIII.

Battle with "the Taxes."—Letter to Miss Pope.—Colman.—
Last Letter to Garrick.—Mr. Cole.—Story of a Foot-
man.—Death of Mrs. Clive.

MR. WALPOLE tells with enjoyment of a conflict which his *friend* got into with the "taxes," and "her tax-gatherer has gone off," he writes, "and she must pay her window-lights over again ; and the road before the door is very bad and the parish won't mend it." How the "combustible" lady took this state of things is related by her neighbour, Miss Hawkins, whose father

"Sir John Hawkins
Without his shoes or *stalkins*,"

was obliged to interfere :

"I remember a reply of the same hue, which she made to two very decent respectful men, then in office as surveyors of the roads in the parish, on my father's sending them to her, as being the acting magistrate of the place, to demand some payment which she had refused:—it was in the laconic terms, "By the living G— I will not pay it." I suppose this might destroy entirely all intercourse with our house, for she was of course compelled to break her oath. I suppose it was to show "what some actresses *can* do— what some *will* do,"—that she worked for the Holbein chamber at Strawberry-hill, the carpet with blue tulips and yellow foliage."

"Mrs. Clive, the comic actress, I believe, by her agreeable or rather diverting society, paid rent for what is called little Strawberry-hill.—Her memory still survives in the place; and her bounty to her indigent relations, is recorded on a tablet affixed to the wall of the church. A virtue less known, and perhaps less easily credited, considering her manners in private, and her cast of characters in public, was her perfect abstinence from spirituous liquors. She told a lady, her neighbour, in Great Queen-street, Lincolu's-Inn-Fields, from whom I had it, that she believed she could say more than most players could, that she never kept any of these exhilarating resources in her house.

"When one of her maid-servants, to whom she had given an admission to see her act, was asked how she liked her mistress on the stage, she said "*she saw no difference between her there and at home.*" It is most probable from this, that the character in which she had seen her, was *Nell* in the farce of "The Devil to Pay."

"I have heard it said that she once attempted *Shylock*, and with the Jewish accent; but the effect was too ludicrous to be endured.

"Mrs. Clive visited my father and mother, but on my mother's running out of the house one evening, when she had called accidentally, to prevent her alighting from her carriage, as the small-pox had made its appearance amongst us and she knew Mrs. Clive not to have had it,—utterly insensible to the politeness of her attention at a moment of such anxiety, she roughly replied, "it was not you I wanted to see it was your husband : *send him out./*"

Miss Pope used to recall her visits to Twickenham to see her friend, and those which Mr. Walpole paid them. He *could* be very agreeable she said, but often "very snarling

and sarcastic." "She was one of my earliest and best
friends," said she, speaking of her dear Clive, "I usually
spent a month with her during the summer recess, at her
cottage. One fine morning I set off in the Twickenham
passage-boat to pay her a visit. When we came to Vauxhall,
I took out a book and read." "Oh ma'am," said one of the
watermen, "I hoped we were to have the pleasure of hearing
you talk." "I took the hint," added the benevolent lady,
"and put up my book." A pleasing good humoured trait.
Not long before Mrs. Clive's death, we find these two old
friends corresponding affectionately.

MRS. CLIVE TO MISS POPE.

"Twickenham, October 17th, 1784.

"My dear Popy. —The jack I must have, and I suppose
the cook will be as much delighted with it, as a fine
lady with a birthday suit. I send you walnuts which are
fine, but pray be moderate in your admiration, for
they are dangerous dainties. John has carried about to my
neighbours above six thousand, and he tells me there
are as many still left, indeed it is a most wonderful
tree. Mrs. Prince has been robbed at two o'clock, at noon,
of her gold watch and four guineas, and at the same
time our two justices of sixpence a-piece ; they had like
to be shott, for not having more. Everybody enquires after
you, and I deliver your compts. Poor Mrs. Hart is dead—
well spoken of by everybody. I pity the poor old Weassel
that is left behind.

Adieu, my dear Popy,

yours ever,

C. CLIVE.

"The jack must carry six or seven and twenty pounds, the
waterman shall bring the money when I know what."

Miss Pope to Mrs. Clive.

"Monday, Feb. 22, 1779.

"Dear Madam.—I have attempted several times to sit
down and answer your very kind letter, and have as often
been interrupted, but at length I am determined you must
know I never think of writing but when I fancy I have
some novelty to relate, and at present only one theme
obtains, which is respecting the admirals. This always ends
in breaking the windows—

"I am much mortified you did not spend Ash Wednesday
with us, as the whole party, I believe, sincerely expected it,
and would have been glad to see you : the Roffeys came
to town on purpose, and inquired after you immediately.
Miss Griffith spent the day with Miss Cadogan, who still
continues to weep for Mr. Garrick, like another Niobe, and
so romantic, it is astonishing : I believe love is at the
bottom with both of them, for that seems the most natural ;
however, they say you are vastly affected, and that you all
wept the other morning like the ladies in 'The Funeral,' and
Mr. Raftor came in like *Counsellor Puzzle* to fill up the
group. I wish I could give you something to laugh at, for
I do not think weeping becoming to you or to me : at least
it should be seldom— . . . What reason you have to
applaud yourself for your conduct : every comfort and every
hour you enjoy, convince me you were right, and I pray
heartily I may tread in your steps (at least in some degree)
to share such a portion of happiness. I am tired with
subscriptions, for (I am sorry to say it) worthless people ;
yet did not one contribute, one would be considered a Bar-
barian. They are setting on foot something of that sort
for Mrs. Bellamy, who is, I hear starving ; she has wearied
everybody with her letters, and is penniless, without food,

fire, or candle—in short nothing can be more wretched :
and I should not be surprised if some ladies in the theatre,
who now carry their heads very high, were reduced some-
time or other, to the same state."

Horace Smith, who knew and admired her, has kept
a pleasing sketch of her.—"Miss Pope's private alias,
in certain theatrical circles, was Mrs. Candour; originating
partly from her playing that part, and partly from her
readiness to undertake the defence of any person who
happened to be run down. I owe it to truth to declare my
conviction that, in adopting that course, not a particle
of irony and sarcasm was mingled with her encomiums.
I never heard her speak ill of any human being. I have
sometimes been even exasperated by her benevolence.   In
cases of the most open delinquency, I could never entice
her into indignation.   "I adore my profession," I have
heard her say more than once.   She had bad health ; she
was attached to a young man who died at Monmouth ; she
is devoted to her sister's children.   She gave an evening
party at her new residence, about a twelvemonth after her
retreat from the stage, at which I remember the late
Mr. Justice Grose was present, as well as a great number of
other highly respectable persons of either sex, many of
them, as I then learned, from the purlieus of St. James's
Palace.   Here I beheld her in society for the last time.
She was shortly afterwards attacked by a stupor of the
brain, and this once lively and amiable woman, who
had entertained me repeatedly with anecdotes of people
of note in her earlier days, sat quietly in an arm-chair
by the fire-side, patting the head of her poodle dog,
and smiling at what passed in conversation, without being
at all conscious of the meaning of what was uttered."

A letter of condolence to sprightly writer, who had given her his Mrs. Heidelburg:—

TO MR. GEORGE COLMAN.
"April 12, 1771.

"SIR.—I hope you heard that I sent my servant to town to inquire how you did; indeed I have been greatly surprised and sincerely concerned for your unexpected distress; there is nothing can be said upon these melancholy occations to a person of understanding. Fools can not feel, people of sense must, and will, and when they have sank their spirits till they are ill, will find that nothing but submission can give any consolation to inevitable misfortunes. I shall be extreamly glad to see you, and think it would be very right, if you would come and dine *hear* two or three days in a week, it will change the *sceen*, and by the sincerity of your wellcome, you may fancy yourself at home.

I am, dearly,
Your obligd. hum. Servt.,
C. CLIVE."

In her retirement we find her old "friend-enemy" Garrick reappearing occasionally. Her letters to him showed, as we before said, what was the regard and affection subsisting between these two sterling natures, now that all cause of friction was removed. Kitty would sometimes rally her old manager in lively fashion, as when she heard he was devoting himself to vestry duties.

MRS. CLIVE TO MR. GARRICK.
"*I schreamed* at your parish business. I think I see you in your churchwardenship quareling for not making those brown loaves big enough; but for God's sake never think of

being a justice of the peace, for the people will quarel on purpose to be brought before you to hear you talk, so that you may have as much business upon the lawn, as you had upon the boards.   If I should live to be thaw'd, I will come to town on purpose to kiss you ; and in the summer, as you say, I hope we shall see each other ten times as often, when we will talk, and dance, and sing, and send our hearers laughing to their beds."

And again :
> "O jealousey thou raging pain,
> Where shall I find my piece again."

"I am in a great fuss.   Pray what is the meaning of a quarter of a hundred of the Miss Moors coming purring about you with their poems, and plays, and romancies ; what, is the Pivy to be roused, and I don't understand it.— Mrs. Garrick has been so good to say she would spare me a little corner of your heart, and I can tell the Miss Moors they shall not have one morsel of it.   *What* do they pretend to take it by *force of lines :* If that's the case I shall write such versses as shall make them stare againe, and send them to Bristol with a flea in their ear !   Here have I two letters, one and not one line, nay, you write to the Poulterer's woman rather than the Pivy, and order her to bring me the note : and the poor creature is so proud of a letter from you, that it has quite turn'd her head, and instead of picking her Poultry ; she is dancing about her shop, with a wisp of straw in her hand, like the poor Ophelia, singing :
> ' How shou'd I your true love know.'

And I must tell you, if you don't write to me directly and tell me a great deal of news, I believe I shall sing the next of the mad songs myself.   I see your run always goes on, which gives me great pleasure—I shall be glad if you will lend it me (Colley Cibber); my love to my dear Mrs. Garrick. I suppose you have had a long letter of thanks from Miss Pope. I have had one from her all over transport. I feel vast happiness about that *afair*, and shall ever remember it as a great obligation you have confered on your, PIVY CLIVE."

Endorsed, " Pivy's letter about Miss Hannah More."

THE SAME TO THE SAME.
"Twickenham, Jan. 13th, 1774.

"DEAR SIR.—I should suppose, when you see Twickenham, you will not presently imagine whom the letter can come from, you have so entirely forgot *me*. I write because I am importuned by the bearer ; and to solicit a great man looks as if one had power, which, you know, is a charming thing. Mr. C—— tells me he knows you very well : he lives at Twickenham, is a wine-merchant, lives in good credit, and has for many years. I have taken my wine of him these four years, which is the reason *he thinks* I ought to trouble you with a letter. He wants to get his son into the excise. He tells me you are at the head of the commission, and can do whatever you please : *you could I know in former days ;* and if you can now, and *will*, Mr. C—— will be very glad of it. I do not know anything of the young man, therefore cannot recommend him, but I suppose his father *can*, for he is a fine chatter box ; he *will be up and tell you* everything about him.

"Pray how does my dear Mrs. Garrick do? for I will love her, because I am sure she would me, if you would let her. But you are a Rudesby (?) yourself, and it is your fault that she does not take notice of me.

. "I might date this letter from the Ark; we are so surrounded with water that it is impossible for any carriage to come to me, or for me to stir out, so that at present my heavenly place is a little develish. I beleive I must win a house in the Adelphi, and come to town in winter: but when I come I shall not have the happiness to see Macklin in "Macbeth." What a pity it is he should make an end of himself in such a *fine part*.

"Your friend Jemmy and Mrs. Mestiver desire their compliments to yourself and Mrs. Garrick, I suppose we shall all meet next summer at Mr. Walpole's.

Adieu, yours ever,
C. CLIVE."

MRS. CLIVE TO MR. GARRICK.
"Twickenham, March 22nd, 1775.

"There is no such being now as Pivy, she has been killed by the cruelty of Garrick; but the Clive thank God is still alive, and alive like to be, and did intend to call you to give an account, for your wicked wishes to her. But having been told of your good deeds and great acting events, I concluded you was in too much conceit with yourself to listen to my complaints. I must needs say that I admire you with the rest of the world, for your great goodness to Miss Moore (More): the protection you gave her play. I daresay she was sensible you were of the greatest service to her; she was sure everything you touched would turn into gold, and though she had great merit in her writing, still your affection for tragedy children was a great happiness to *her*, for you dandled it and fondled it, and then carried it in your arms to town, to nurse. Who behaved so kindly to it that it run alone in a month.

"I must now mention the noblest action of your life, your generosity to nephew David; all the world is repeating your praises. The people who always envied you and wished to detract from you, always declaring you loved money too much, ever to part from it, now they will *feel* foolish, and look contemptible : all that I can say is, *I wish that heaven had made me such an uncle.*

"I hope my dear Mrs. Garrick is perfect well ; happy she must ever be ; she has a disposition which will make her so in all situations. You and I, you know, can alter our tempers with the weathercock. We are all here at present but queer. Mrs. Mastivre is not sick (but sorry); your Jemsey is nither one thing nor the other—always dreaming of Garrick and the opera.

" Everybody is raving against Mr. Sheridan for his supineness. The country is very dull : we have not twenty people in the village, but still it is better than London. Let me see you—let me hear from you : and tell me all the news you can to divert your ever affectionate and forgiving

C. CLIVE.'

Our brother and sister join in compliments to your lady and self.

MR. GARRICK TO MRS. CLIVE.

" Hampton, Friday Morning.

" Has not the nasty bile which so often confines, and has heretofore tormented you, kept me at home, I should have been at your feet three days ago. If your heart (wonderful combustible like my own!) has played off all the squibs and rockets which lately occasioned a little cracking and bouncing about me, and can receive again the more gentle and pleasing fireworks of love and friendship,

I will be with you at six this evening, to revive by the help
of those spirits in your tea kettle lamp, that flame which
was almost blown out by the flouncing of your petticoat,
when my name was mentioned. . . .   Can my Pivy know
so little of me, to think that I prefer the clack of Lords
and Ladies, to the enjoyment of humour and genius? . . .
In short your misconceptions about that fête Champêtre
(devil take the word) has made me so cross about everything
that belongs to it, that I curse all squibs, crackers, rockets,
air balloons, mines, serpents, and catherine wheels ; and can
think of nothing, and wish for nothing, but laugh, gig,
humour, fun, pun, conundrum, carri witchet, and Catherine
Clive.   I am ever, my Pivy's most constant and loving,
D. GARRICK."

MRS. CLIVE TO MR. GARRICK.

"Twickenhem, January 23rd, 1774.

"WONDERFUL SIR.— Who have been for thirty years
contradicting an old established proverb, 'you cannot make
bricks without straw ;' but you have done what is infinitely
more difficult, for you have made actors and actresses without genius, that is you have made them pass for *such*,
which has answered your end, though it has given you
infinite trouble.   You never took much pains with yourself
for you could not help acting well, therefore I do not think
you have much merrit in that, though to be sure it has
been very assuaging to yourself, as well as the rest of
the world ; for while you are laughing at your own conceits,
you was at the same time sure they would cram your iron
chests.   What put the fancy in my head, was your desiring
a good character of young Crofts.   It is a sad thing some
people would say, that such a paltry being as an exciseman,

cannot get his bread unless he has behaved well in the world ; and yet it is so perfectly right, that everybody would have the same caution, not to give good characters when they did not deserve them, nor receive people into your family for servants, or any kind of business, who had them not. If this was made an unalterable rule, the world must in time become *all* sorts of good people.

"I send the enclosed, which may be depended on. Mr. Costard is our rector, one of the most learned and best sort of men in the world. They say he has more knowledge in the stars, and among all the sky-people than anybody, so that most of us take him for a conjuror. I ought to make an apology for being so troublesome, when I come to town I will make my excuse, when I shall at the same time see Mrs. Garrick, which will always be a real pleasure to dear sir,

Yours,

C. PIVY."

The spirit and vivacity of these epistles will strike every one, and they deservedly excited the admiration of that accomplished critic, Mr. John Forster.

To the very last the spirited actress sustained her humour. When some Jewish visitors excused them from going to see Strawberry Hill, as the day was one of their Feast, she suggested that "they should change their religion"—a happy compliment moreover to the host. In 1766, when Lady Shelburne was coming to Twittenham, "you know," Walpole wrote, "Lady Suffolk is *deaf*, and I have talked much of a charming old person I have met at Paris—Madm. Du Deffand —who is *blind*. " Well," said Clive, "if the new Countess is but *lame*, I shall have no chance of ever seeing you."

No wonder he designed some venison for "the *demidium
animæ meæ*, Mrs. Clive (a pretty round half,)" he adds.
His letters, indeed, quite help us to follow her in that sleepy
district until her death—and a very pleasant sketch they
furnish. Thus in 1773; "except being extremely ill, Mrs.
Clive is extremely well. The papers said she was to act
at Covent Garden.* She has printed a very proper answer
in the *Evening Post.*" When he invited a lady of quality
down, Mrs. Clive was held out as an attraction :

TO LADY CECILIA JOHNSTONE.

Aug. 19, 1777.

Our abdicated monarch Lear,
And bonny Dame Cadwallader,
With a whole Theatre from France,
And Raftor, wont th' eclipse in Hays to dance,
Next Saturday, if fair or foul,
On bacon, ham, and chicken fowl,
Intend with Horace—no great bard,
In one of Epicurus herd,
To dine.

Mr. Cole, a laborious antiquarian, whose notes and
diaries fill many volumes, once in 1779, paid a visit to
Mr. Walpole, and gives this account of what he saw :
"Mrs. Clive, the celebrated actress and comedian, has
a little box contiguous to Mr. Walpole's garden, and
close almost to the chapel.   Here she lives retired and
her brother, Mr. Raftor, with her, but he was not disposed

---

* When Mr. and Mrs. Bancroft revived "Masks and Faces," at
the Haymarket Theatre, Miss Wade, who performed the part of
Mrs. Clive, used Kitty's own walking stick. It had a china crutch
top, and was a present from Walpole to Mrs. Damer, from whom it
passed to my friend Mr. Campbell Johnstone.

to stir out.   **** While I was at Strawberry Hill, I saw
on the table a scrap of paper, with the following verses
on Mrs. Clive, which I took a copy of, though I had
no leave from Mr. Walpole for so doing; yet as they
lay publicly for anyone to see them, I thought it no breach
of honour to copy them.   They seemed to me, from the
blotting and alterations of the writing, to have been lately
composed,   probably   the   evening   before,   while   Mrs.
Clive was present, and meant as a sportive and innocent
amusement, to divert the time.   They were written by way
of epitaph, and on a supposition that Mrs Clive was
dead."

Her footman was recommended to her through an odd
adventure.   A retired officer, Captain Prescott, who had
married a young wife, used to treat her with such violence
that his servant left him, and was engaged by Mrs. Clive.
When the young lady could endure it no longer, he assisted
her to elope.   As some legal proceedings followed, he was
examined, and when Lord Manfield asked him severely how
he could do such a thing, replied " that his late master would
have murdered his wife—so he had done him a service in
saving him from being hanged !" an answer that delighted
all at " Twittenham," and Mrs. Clive specially.

In December, 1780, the actress learned the death of her
husband, Mr. George Clive, at a great age, who had now
been separated from her nearly fifty years.   He had long
since retired to Bath, to enjoy the easy competence bequeathed to him by his friend Ince, of " Spectator " memory,
and according to the effusive testimony of the obituary
notices, was lamented as " a gentleman of extensive learning
and one of the first classical scholars of the age :" while
" his philosophic disposition " enabled him to support his

"various afflictions with a resignation which evinced his goodness of heart." He was esteemed and "visited by Mr. Melmoth," and "all the *literati* thought themselves honoured by his acquaintance." It was added that he owed much to the teachings of "that great master of all literature, Dr. Snape," on the mere "mention of whose name *he ever paid the grateful tribute of a sigh.*" If Mr. George Clive was indeed such a paragon, it is to be feared that the blame of the separation must be laid to the account of the fractious and less perfect Kitty.

In 1782, she had serious attacks of illness, and her old friend thought she could not survive. "I thought her in a bad way, her house is little less than an infirmary." In August, "poor Mrs. Clive is certainly very declining, but has been better of late; and, what I am glad of, thinks herself better." But in September, she rallied, "Dame Cliveden is the only heroine among all us old Dowagers; she is so much recovered, she ventures to go out cruising on all the neighbours," and in October, he could write, "Mrs. Cliveden, I flatter myself is nearly recovered, having had no relapses since. She even partakes of the carnival, which at Twickenham, commences at Michaelmas, and lasts as long as there are four persons to make a pool. I am to go to her this evening for what she calls *only two tables.*"

In July, 1783, she had her favourite Miss Pope with her. "Pope has been at Mrs. Clive's this week. I wrote a line of excuse, but hoped very soon to salute Miss Pope's eye."

But, at last the intrepid old actress had to succumb :

"My poor old friend is a great loss. I had played cards with her at Mrs. Gostlings, three nights before I came to town, and found her extremely confused, and not knowing what she did, indeed I had perceived something of the sort before, and had found her much broken this autumn. It seems that the day after, she went to General Lister's burial, and got cold, and has been ill for two or three days. On the Wednesday morning, she rose to have her bed made, with her maid by her, sunk down at once, and died without a pang or a groan. Her brother took the loss sadly to heart—poor Mr. Raftor is shrunk to the greatest degree, and for some days would not see anybody. I sent for him to town to me, but he will not come till next week."

Her death occurred on December 6th, 1785. Her old friend set up an urn in his gardens, to her memory—a testimonial then in fashion—with this inscription :—

> " Ye smiles and jests still hover round ;
> This is mirth's consecrated ground.
> Here lived the laughter loving dame,
> A matchless actress, Clive her name.
> The comic muse with her retired,
> And shed a tear when she expired."*

The old church at Twickenham, is a quaint and comfortable structure of genial red brick, with a burly air, and pleasantly situated on the river bank, in its own churchyard. Walking round it, we find on the outside

---

* On which the venomous Walcot addressed some lines

TO MR. HORACE WALPOLE.

On his inscription on an urn dedicated to Mrs. Clive,

BY PETER PINDAR, ESQ.

Horace of Strawberry Hill, I mean not Rome,
Lo ! all thy geese are swans I do presume—
Truth and thy trumpet seem not to agree :
Know comedy is heart,—all alive—
The sprightly lass no more expired with Clive,
Then Dame humility will die with thee."

wall, in an obscure corner at the back, a poorish, rather
starved looking tablet, fixed against the wall, not a couple
of feet square.   This is the memorial to the famous actress,
set up by Miss Pope, and which could not have cost her
friend more than a couple of pounds.

SACRED TO THE MEMORY OF

MRS. CATHERINE CLIVE,

WHO DIED DECEMBER 6TH, 1785,

AGED 75 YEARS.

This meagre memorial is however embellished by some
indifferent verses, the composition of her sorrowing friend.

The faithful "Jemmy" Raftor did not long survive his
gifted sister.   He died on September 30th, 1790, leaving
behind him the reputation of a jovial, humorous creature,
but of an indifferent performer.   A friend recalled one last
touch of character:—"We remember," he says, with that
tone of good-natured contempt which ever follows the
Viveur, "her acting *Bayes* in 'The Rehearsal' with her
brother, a very inferior actor, speaking (as usual) like a
mouse in a cheese, in the character of *bold Thunder !*   'O
fie, Mr. Raftor," said she, 'speak out like a man.   Surely
you might have learned more assurance from your sister !'"
This was characteristic, and presents a happy sketch of
brother and sister.

Our actress was something of an authoress, and her
native vivacity, as we have seen, found vent in several
light productions, pamphlets, controversial letters, and a
few "pieces of occasion,"—Among these were "Bayes in
Petticoats," already described,* "Every Woman in her
Humour," "Sketch of a Fine Lady's Return from a Rout,"
"The Island of Slaves," a translation—attributed to her
on doubtful authority.   She was never tired of ridiculing
ladies of extravagant fashion, though she must have had
no opportunities of studying their weaknesses, for she was
not likely to have been admitted to their society.   The
same lack of opportunities must vitiate all attempts to
pourtray the follies of the upper classes—the mere palpable
absurdities of dress and bearing being all the stock-in-trade
that is available.

CONCLUSION.

Such was Catherine Clive—whose character, as well as
whose performances have enriched the associations of literature, besides increasing the gaiety of the nation.   As will
have been seen from this trifling record, she was an interesting
woman, straightforward and honorable in her character—
bright, gay, and good-natured.   We recall her image with
pleasure—even her little *boutades:* we could ill spare
her from the histrionic ranks, for she was an actress of the
first rank, well deserving the handsome encomium of Goldsmith, who had seen the leading performers of Europe.
"She has more true humour," he wrote, "than any actress
upon the English or any other stage I have seen." '

---

* In his article in the "National Biography," Sir T. Martin gives
this piece as " *Boys* in Petticoats,"—a diverting mistake.